AUDITING JANE DOE

A CYNTHIA WEBBER NOVEL

MICHELLE CORNISH

Published in Canada by SolVin Creative.

This novel is set in Canada, written by a Canadian, and therefore, uses Canadian spelling.

Auditing Jane Doe is a work of fiction. Names, characters, places, and incidents either are products of the author's imagination or are used fictitiously. Any resemblance to actual events or people (living or dead) is entirely coincidental.

Cover design by DeeVA Global

Editing and proofreading services provided by Bobbi Beatty, Silver Scroll Services

ISBN 978-1775083658

Discover other titles by Michelle Cornish at

www.michellecornish.com

Cynthia Webber

Murder Audit (Book 1)

Non-fiction

Keep More Money

Prosperity Planner

Freeing the Butterfly

To Scott, for knowing I'm crazy but supporting and loving me anyway.

ACKNOWLEDGMENTS

A special thanks to my beta readers: Angel, Kay, Kris, Lindsay, Mark, Nicole, Scott, Siobhan, and Sue. Your feedback was invaluable and made *Auditing Jane Doe* much better.

To Constable Mark Smith and Calgary Police Services, thank you for taking the time to answer my questions.

1

Cynthia sprinted for the main entrance of Ben's building, hoping someone would see her and hold the door. A giant bag of Chinese food she'd picked up after work filled both hands. Chinese food had seemed like a great way to celebrate. But a hot sticky mess had formed on the hand supporting the bottom of the bag, and the last thing she wanted was to balance the mess against her crisp white blouse so she could buzz Ben's apartment.

She saw a woman in a purple raincoat and a man about six feet tall entering the building several metres ahead of her.

"Hold the door, please!" she yelled as loud as she could over the traffic on the street. The couple either didn't hear her or chose to ignore her, and the door closed as Cynthia shoved her foot in front of it. The door was heavier than she remembered, and it knocked her off balance as it smashed into her back.

Trapped in the doorway with no free hands, she had no choice but to hug the Chinese food tight to her chest as the space between the door and its frame shrunk. She looked for the couple she had seen entering the building and frowned, realizing they were nowhere to be seen. How could they have caught the elevator so quickly?

She pushed back on the door, trying to make room to pass through, but it felt like her shoulder bag was stuck on something. Then she felt the door get much lighter, and she stumbled backwards into a young woman with short dark hair.

"Sorry," she said, glancing over her shoulder at the woman who seemed about twenty-five, ten years her junior.

"No worries." The woman looked Cynthia up and down. "Do

you need a hand? Can I take something for you?"

"I think I'm all right now," Cynthia said, afraid to remove the bag of Chinese food from her chest and assess the damage.

Both women headed for the elevator. It arrived almost as soon as the dark-haired woman pressed the up button. They stepped in and the dark-haired woman pressed the button for the penthouse.

"What floor?" she asked Cynthia.

"Seven, thanks."

The smell of fresh Chinese food filled the elevator, and Cynthia was relieved she wasn't the one going all the way to the penthouse. Her stomach was churning and rumbling, and she hoped Ben had set the table and remembered the wine. The elevator stopped on the seventh floor.

"Thanks again," Cynthia said, glancing back at the woman as she left the elevator.

"No problem." The woman looked up from her phone and shot her a quick wave.

The door to Ben's apartment opened almost as soon as Cynthia was off the elevator, and Ben stepped out.

"There you are," he said. "I was just coming downstairs to look for you." He held the door open for Cynthia. "Let me take that for you," he said, gesturing at the bag of Chinese food.

Cynthia reluctantly handed the bag to Ben. "Careful," she said. "The bottom of the bag's about to burst."

Ben put a hand under Cynthia's and she slid hers out. She felt her shirt sticking to her and looked down to see sauce smears on it. Ben put the food on the counter and turned back to Cynthia.

"Great," she said, looking at the stain on her shirt while plopping her shoulder bag down on the floor.

"Looks like you could use a clean shirt," Ben said, taking a step towards her and planting a peck on her lips. "Let me help you with that," he said, unbuttoning her shirt and slipping her blouse off her shoulders. He caressed her hair and kissed her again, this time deeper and longer. Her shirt fell to the floor.

"Mmmm," he said, breaking away from the kiss. "How was your day?"

"Much better, thank you," she said, smiling. Ben grabbed her hand and tried to lead her to his bedroom.

"Let me just soak my shirt," she said, resisting his pull.

"Really? Clearly I need to work on my moves if your shirt is your priority."

"Sorry," she said, picking up her shirt and laying it on the counter.

"Your shirt can wait. I'll soak it for you when we're done. Hell, I'll buy you a new one."

Cynthia laughed. What was she thinking? Laundry over her hunk of a boyfriend? Being a single mom for the last two years had made her far too practical.

2

It was a beautiful night in the city. The lights sparkled, and the spring temperature was just right for dinner on the roof. Vivian had been right about that. Dinner had been amazing. If she hadn't seen it with her own eyes, she wouldn't have believed Vivian had cooked it herself.

But now, none of that mattered. Now, the dark-haired woman was in trouble. Big trouble. And Vivian was just sitting there while she was forced against the safety rail by this vile man. How could she just sit there and not do anything? It probably wouldn't matter anyway.

He had a gun.

"Take off your clothes," he ordered. The gun was inches from the brunette's face. She glared directly into his eyes as she unbuttoned her blouse, spending as long as she could on each button, trying to think of a way out of this mess. Pressed as she was against the rail, she looked over her shoulder at the street below. It was so far down. The cool air touched her cheeks. "Don't get any ideas," he warned. "There's nowhere for you to go."

As she stripped down to her bra and panties, she closed her eyes, wishing she could escape to somewhere else. Anywhere. The hair on her arms rose in response to the spring air.

He stepped closer to her, and she felt his hot breath in her face. Then the cold, hard metal of the gun touched her skin, and her eyes jolted open, wordlessly pleading with her assaulter. He leaned in and tried to kiss her. She fought as hard as she could to turn away, but the gun barrel dug deeper into the side of her neck. She gave in.

"See, that's not so bad." He trailed the tip of the gun down between her breasts. "This too," he said, fondling her bra with his gun. "I want it all off. Nothing but skin."

Still glaring at him, she mentally flipped him the bird. Doing it for real might end her life, and she wasn't ready to do that yet. By the time her bra and panties were in a pile at her feet, he had his fly undone. He grabbed her wrist and forced her to feel his swollen dick. She closed her eyes, trying to numb herself, trying to leave her body. Then he pressed his groin into hers, and pinned her to the railing again.

From the table they'd dined at earlier, she could hear Vivian finally pleading with him to stop. But *she* wished he would just get it over with already. She just wanted to put this whole night behind her.

"Jesus Christ," he said over his shoulder. "Shut . . . Up." She felt his fiery breath again for a second, and then she sensed him step back. Cold air rushed in to replace him. She opened her eyes. Her breath caught at what she saw. Vivian had left the table and was stomping towards them.

"I'm not going to sit here and let you do this," she said, pointing her finger at him like she was scolding a child. She was crying again and looking at the brunette. "I'm so sorry. Sorry for everything."

As Vivian stepped within striking distance, he lashed out and backhanded her across the face with his gun, sending her to the ground.

"Nooooo! Vivian!" The dark-haired woman shrieked at the top of her lungs, then screamed for help, suddenly released from the trance he'd held her in.

"Shut. Up. Why won't you women listen to me?" He tried to cover her mouth and she swung at his hands, trying to bat them away. She thrust her knee up, hoping it would hit him in the groin hard enough to make him double over. Instead, he caught her ankle in his grip and shoved her as hard as he could over the rail.

He did up his fly and strolled over to where Vivian had landed. She looked like a life-sized rag doll, all dressed up. "You're welcome," he said as he stepped over her and continued to the door.

***

Cynthia and Ben sat on the couch in his tiny apartment. After reheating the Chinese food, they were finally eating and celebrating. They were officially professional accountants. It was a day Cynthia had felt would never come.

She rolled up the sleeve on Ben's robe so it wouldn't drag through the food on her plate as she ate. Ben took a sip of wine.

Booonnggggg-ooonngggg!

A loud gonging reverberated off the balcony railing outside. The vibrations continued as Cynthia and Ben looked at each other, then towards the balcony.

"You heard that, right?" Cynthia asked, frowning as she glanced from the direction of the sound back to Ben.

"Yeah. What was it? I've never heard anything like that. My ears are still ringing." Ben stood and hurried towards the balcony doors as Cynthia braced herself on the couch, fearful someone was on the balcony even though she knew that was impossible. How on earth would they get to the seventh floor? It had sounded like someone had taken a large sledgehammer and slammed it against the metal railing.

Ben slid the glass door open, and the full-length curtains followed him out onto the balcony. There was nothing there, so he leaned over to have a look below.

"What the fff . . . ?" said Ben.

Cynthia jumped up, but Ben was already on his way back inside.

"Don't go out there."

"What's going on? Did something hit the balcony?"

All the colour had drained from Ben's face. He seemed to be processing what he had seen below. After what seemed like an eternity, Ben spoke. "I think it's . . . a body."

"What?! A body?"

"Yeah. I'm going downstairs. See if I can find out what's going on." Ben gave her arm a squeeze then headed for the door.

"Do you think they're okay?" Cynthia knew the answer, but hoped she was wrong. Ben looked at her and shook his head.

"We're seven floors up," he said, raising his eyebrows.

"Should I call 911?"

Ben put on his runners and reached for the doorknob. "Let me check it out. Maybe it just *looks* like a body. I've got my cell."

The door closed behind Ben, leaving Cynthia alone in his apartment. She stood there for a moment just staring at the door. Just minutes ago they'd been celebrating, and now . . .

She took a deep breath and crept to the balcony. The sliding door was still open, and the curtains billowed into the living room. It reminded Cynthia of a creepy scene from a movie. She'd meant to slide the door closed but found herself walking out onto the balcony instead.

Keeping a tight grip on the railing, she peered over the edge, revealing nothing but darkness and the reflection of the streetlights as they danced off the pool in the common area below. She scanned the black perimeter of the common area, paying particular attention to the corner beneath a neighbouring balcony.

There it was, on the darkest patch of grass. How had it landed so close to the corner? Cynthia didn't know if it was the night shadows or the adrenaline racing through her veins, but the body looked naked.

Sirens blared, and flashlight beams cut the darkness, bringing movement to the ground near the body as emergency personnel did their jobs. There was nothing Cynthia could do. She turned and went back inside, closing the door behind her.

3

The sound of the body hitting Ben's balcony still rang in Cynthia's ears. It was all she could focus on as she sat on the couch waiting for Ben to come back. Did they jump? Were they pushed? How did she never realize there was access to the roof of Ben's forty-floor building?

Ben seemed to be taking forever to come back. She wanted to go check on him, but he'd made it clear she was to wait. Fighting the urge to go to the lobby, she decided she'd give him a few more minutes. She changed out of Ben's robe into her pants and one of Ben's t-shirts. Now, she needed a distraction.

Her gaze landed on the CPA magazine on the coffee table as she walked back into the living room. It was folded open to the page featuring this season's top three exam writers. Seeing her face on the page made all her hard work as a student and single mom seem worth it, but none of that mattered right now. She was sure Ben wasn't in any danger, but the shock of what had just happened made her nervous. Maybe the TV would make a good distraction.

She found the remote and pushed the red button. "Gah!" Cynthia screamed and jumped back on the couch. Ben had been blasting the music channel. She silenced the music and scrolled for something to watch. She saw the familiar face of her best friend, Linda Reeves, an investigative reporter for S-CAL, a South Calgary news station. She paused on the channel. Cynthia always enjoyed Linda's stories. She was a fair reporter who wasn't afraid to cover controversial issues.

"You have quite the mess to sort out, Miss Bosche. Where do you plan to start?" Linda showed no qualms about getting straight to the point. She had been personally involved in the Prairie Pipeline Company mess too. If it hadn't been for Linda's investigative skills, Cynthia didn't know where she and her family would be right now. Before she could let the memories of the PPC murders get to her, she focused her attention back on the TV and Linda's interview.

Trudy Bosche appeared professional and business-like. She and Linda were standing in front of PPC's main office just south of the city. The two women were evenly matched at about five foot eight. Trudy's hair was cut short, and she wore a plain grey pant suit. Linda, on the other hand, looked like a younger version of her idol, Diane Sawyer. She wore a red blouse with a black suit jacket and knee-length skirt.

Cynthia couldn't help but think how rare it was for a pipeline company to have a female CFO, as much as she hated to admit it. In most of her dealings with oil and gas audits, Cynthia found herself dealing with men.

"Yes, Miss Reeves. It seems I do have quite the mess to clean up. Prairie Pipeline Company is fortunate that messes are what I do best." Bosche flashed a sly smile. "I want the citizens of Calgary to know they haven't seen the last of PPC. While construction on the Rocky Mountain Pipeline ceased during investigations related to events surrounding my predecessor, we are on track to resume construction next week."

Cynthia was surprised it had taken PPC this long to get back up and running. It had been a few months since they'd first shut down. She checked her phone. Ben's five minutes was up.

Whoosh-bang!

Cynthia jumped as the apartment door slammed shut. She leapt off the couch and turned around to see Ben entering the living room, his face as white as a ghost. He looked at Cynthia and froze, as if physically unable to express what he was feeling. She walked over to Ben and grabbed his hands in hers. "Everything okay?" she whispered, already knowing the answer.

"I . . ."

"Come and sit down," Cynthia said, leading him to the couch. "Do you want some water?"

"I'm going to need something a lot stronger than that. I mean, I know we live in a city with over a million other people . . ." he paused to catch his breath. "But I never imagined I'd see something like that." He rubbed his hands through his golden-brown hair before looking up at Cynthia.

"Do you want to talk about it?" Cynthia asked.

"Not really, but I probably should." Ben rested his elbows on his knees and held his head in his hands.

"What did you see?"

"By the time I got down to the lobby, there were already quite a few people there. Detective Bain was outside with two other officers and the body." Ben released his head from his hands and let out a huff of air.

"The EMTs were out there too, but I don't think there was anything anyone could have done," he said. Cynthia held one of Ben's hands in both of hers while he talked. He paused often while he described what he'd seen downstairs.

"It's okay," Cynthia said, feeling useless. "Let me get you that drink. What do you want?" She picked up the empty wine bottle from the coffee table as she stood and headed for the kitchen.

"I think there's some tequila in the cupboard above the fridge."

"You got it," Cynthia said, grabbing the bottle and pouring a shot. "I don't see any limes though."

Ben chuckled in spite of the situation. "Very funny. Real men don't need lime."

"I didn't realize you were a real man," Cynthia said, walking back to the couch and attempting a wink that ended up looking more like she was having issues with her contact lens. Ben mimed a hit to the heart, and Cynthia handed him the shot glass.

"Ouch." He said before downing the tequila in one easy gulp. "Ahhh." He took another deep breath and slowly let it all out.

An uncomfortable silence hung in the air while Cynthia

contemplated what to say next. Of course, there was no way anyone could survive a fall like that. "Did anyone know who—"

Ben anticipated Cynthia's question and shook his head. "There was a lot of chatter but no names."

Cynthia paused, unsure how to ask her next question. "Did you . . . see . . . the body?" Her voice softened as she asked.

"Not really. I could see a foot from where I was standing, but I was inside looking out, so I'm not even sure if that's what I saw. It looked like a woman's foot."

"How could you tell?"

"I thought I saw a tattoo. A rose. Not a lot of men have rose tattoos on their feet."

"Fair enough," Cynthia agreed, feeling the solemnness of the situation sink in. She thought about her son, Luke, and how it was getting close to his bedtime, but she didn't want to leave Ben alone.

"Looks like my neighbour," Ben gestured air quotes at the word 'neighbour,' "might be the talk of your office tomorrow. If the victim was someone who lives here. I guess it could have been anyone who had access to the roof."

Ben glanced at the TV still playing in the background. As if the shock of the situation had suddenly lifted, he looked back at her and said, "Oh, shit. I'm sorry. You probably need to get back home to Luke."

"I can call my mom and see if she can stay longer."

"It's okay."

"Are you going to be all right? You could stay at my place if you want?"

Ben's lips curled into a wicked smile and Cynthia couldn't help but think how green his eyes looked in the dim light of his living room.

"That's sweet, but I'll be fine," Ben replied, getting up to walk Cynthia to the door. Cynthia strolled into the kitchen and grabbed her stained blouse from the counter before stuffing it in her shoulder bag on her way to the door. "This was definitely not the romantic celebration I'd planned," Ben said, bending down to kiss Cynthia. "Text me when you get home."

He squeezed her tight before letting her walk out the door.

4

Thinking about the horrible noise she'd heard as the body hit Ben's balcony made it difficult for Cynthia to sleep. She wandered into the living room where her phone sat on the coffee table. She tried calling Detective Bain to see if he had any details, but his voicemail kicked in without so much as a ring. Even though she worked in the financial crimes department as a forensic accountant, there was always a lot of talk between departments, especially when a new case came in.

She tossed her phone on the couch beside her and it buzzed. There was only a handful of people who would call this late. Her instincts told her it was Linda.

"Hi. I'm so glad you called. You aren't going to believe what happened at Ben's tonight."

"You're forgetting who you're talking to," said Linda.

"Right." Cynthia rolled her eyes and shook her head. Of course, Linda would have already heard the news.

"There are some advantages to working in a newsroom. I don't know everything though. Just that someone jumped. I didn't realize it was at Ben's building."

"Yeah, the body hit Ben's balcony on the way down. It sounded so horrible. I can still hear it."

"That's awful. Do you want me to come over?"

"I'll be all right. What's up?"

"I was just calling to let you know I'll be stopping by the station tomorrow. I know how Detective Bain is about your best friend being a reporter, so I thought I should warn you."

"Yes, he *is* a stickler for doing things by the book. Thanks for letting me know. Do I want to know why you'll be stopping by?"

"I need to badger the good detective for a statement about a missing woman. Her mother's been pestering me, saying the police aren't doing anything. She told me some things that might help the case. I just want to make sure Detective Bain has all the details. I'm not sure this woman trusts him."

"And what do *you* think?" Cynthia reminded herself to keep her voice down, so she didn't wake her four-year old.

"I think the good detective does the best he can, but it seems like he's short-staffed, just like every other employer in this city."

"That's true. I'm pretty sure I only got my job because Louise was desperate for help."

"That and you're a damn good accountant," Linda said. "I don't want to say too much over the phone, but I think either you or Louise are going to want to hear what I have to say tomorrow."

"Is it Amarillis Kane?" Cynthia asked. "The missing woman you need to ask Detective Bain about? I've heard him talk about the case a bit."

"Yes, it's about Maris. Her mom gave me a notebook. There are some pretty serious statements about Cooper Downs in there."

"The racetrack?"

"Yeah. Maris worked in the accounting department there."

"You know I always look forward to seeing you. Even if it's business. I love that I get to see you while I'm at work now." Cynthia beamed, though her friend couldn't see her.

"See you tomorrow, Cyn."

Cynthia thought about what Linda had said, coming up with her own scenarios as to what might be in the notebook. She'd been following the missing person's case. It was hard not to. Amarillis Kane was the assistant Horsemen's Bookkeeper at Cooper Downs Racetrack and Casino, and she'd been missing for weeks. There must be some sort of financial fraud implications in the notebook if Linda thought she and Louise needed to see it.

Excitement rose in her belly, making it even more difficult for her to settle in to sleep. She loved solving the puzzles financial crimes provided. Even though she'd only been with the Calgary police for three months, she'd already seen how greed and desperation made people do unthinkable things.

5

Detective Randy Bain arrived at his darkened bungalow in the suburbs of northeast Calgary just after 1:00 a.m. Exhausted from the night's events, he was looking forward to seeing his yellow lab, Boomer. He parked his car in the driveway and sat for a moment, reflecting on the increased number of suicides in the city over the last few months.

Finally, he pushed himself out of his car and trudged up to his front door. He put his key in the lock and tried to empty his mind of all the work-related details floating around in there. Boomer barked from the other side of the door, and Randy was sure Boomer was bouncing up and down as he often did when Randy arrived home.

"Hey, Boo," he said as he crossed the threshold and, without removing his boots or coat, walked across the living room to let Boomer out into the backyard so he could do his business. Then he took off his boots and hung his coat in the entryway closet. Boomer let out a quiet bark indicating he was ready to come back inside.

"Who's a good boy?" Randy said, ruffling Boomer's ears. "We'll go for a walk in the morning." Boomer's ears perked at the word "walk". It was clear he wanted to go right now, but all Randy wanted to do was sleep. After a moment of contemplation, he opted for a beer instead.

He padded his way to the fridge. The pile of mail he'd left on the counter earlier in the day taunted him. He'd been adding to it over the last couple of weeks, not wanting to deal with the bills. Randy pried the cap off his beer as he let out a long sigh then rubbed the reddish-brown stubble on his chin. He grabbed the pile of mail and sat down at the kitchen table. Boomer rested his head on Randy's lap, using his upturned eyes to try and will his owner to go for that walk.

By the time Randy was done opening his mail, he'd counted at least half a dozen past due notices, all from different creditors, but it was the last notice that had hit him the hardest. The bank was threatening to repossess his home. He'd worked his ass off as a young officer and was proud he'd become a homeowner before any of his peers. The regret he felt for letting things get this bad hung over him like a rain cloud waiting to burst.

"Jesus, Boomer, I've sure made a mess of things," he said, scratching Boomer's ear. He took a swig of his amber ale, picked up his phone, and pressed the speed dial.

"I'm ready to make a deal."

"I knew you'd come around." The voice on the other end was smooth yet too cocky for Randy's liking. "Meet me at the casino tomorrow."

The casino. Just hearing the word caused the hair on the nape of Randy's neck to stand up and his blood to rush a little faster through his veins. He wouldn't be in this mess if it wasn't for that damn casino.

Randy hung up and looked at his faithful companion. "Oh, Boo. I know what you're thinking, but it's the only way." His companion wagged his tail and nudged Randy with his nose as if to ask, "Walk now?"

6

Cynthia hadn't slept much, and though she was a bit fuzzy-headed, she was still excited to get to work. After being wrongfully dismissed by her former boss while working on the financial statement audit for PPC, she'd decided not to pursue a lawsuit. There were other circumstances related to her dismissal that led her to believe she would be happier working with the police anyway. She enjoyed the challenge of following a paper trail to catch the bad guy.

After finding a body while counting inventory at PPC, Cynthia had gotten to know Detective Bain. He'd been impressed with Cynthia's discoveries relating to the PPC case and offered her a job working for the police in the financial crimes department. Cynthia had been happy to take the job and forget about the unfortunate events surrounding her former employer, Darlington & Associates accounting firm. While Linda had urged her to pursue the wrongful dismissal, the idea had stressed Cynthia out. A fresh start with the Calgary police was just what she'd needed. She was happy she had a job to support herself and Luke.

Cynthia arrived at the station after dropping Luke off with her parents for the day. Once in her office, she took a salad out of her brown bag lunch and headed to the staff room to put it in the fridge. Then she strode a couple doors down the hall from her office to see if Randy was in. When she got to his open door, she saw him lift a coffee cup to his lips and move some papers that had been resting under it only to place his cup on top of other papers. An interesting filing system. It was a wonder all his paperwork didn't end up with coffee stains on it.

"Detective, do you have a minute?" Cynthia said, peering into his office. It was important to her to warn him Linda would be stopping by to talk about Maris Kane's case rather than have him assume Linda was attempting to grab information she could report on the air. Linda played by the book most of the time, but other reporters had tarnished the press's reputation with the detective, and he often became irritated when they showed up unexpectedly.

"Good morning, Cynthia. How many times do I have to tell you to call me Randy? You've been here almost three months now." Because Randy was the detective who'd interviewed her after she'd found the body at PPC, she still thought of him more as Detective Bain than Randy, her boss.

"Sorry . . . Randy."

"What's up?"

"Linda's going to be stopping by with some evidence for the Amarillis Kane case. I'll let her fill you in on the details. All I know is she's got a journal Maris's mom found." The puzzled look on Randy's face told Cynthia he wanted more info. "Linda thinks there's something in the journal that implicates Cooper Downs in some financial fraud." Randy's expression lightened. "Maybe something in the journal will help find Maris," Cynthia added.

"I admire your optimism. Thanks for the heads up." Randy looked down at his notes then back at Cynthia. "I saw your boyfriend, Ben, last night at his apartment. He seemed pretty shaken up. Were you there too?"

"Unfortunately. The sound of that body hitting the balcony was awful. I've never heard anything like it, so loud and looming." She paused, the horrible vibration still fresh in her mind. Sure Randy had seen and heard much worse, but unsure how much more she should say, she continued. "I didn't sleep much before Luke got up." Then a horrible thought crossed her mind. "Any chance that was Maris?" Why she hadn't thought of this sooner?

"I had been hopeful the description matched Maris's," Randy

said. "Shit, that sounds awful, but most missing persons cases don't end well . . . if we even find them at all."

"I understand." Cynthia looked down at the floor, reflecting, pausing for the victims who were never found. "It's not Maris then?" Her eyes met Randy's in anticipation.

"No, Maris is a redhead with long hair. A pretty feisty one too, according to the friends I've interviewed. She's about the same size as our Jane Doe, but Jane Doe's got short dark hair and a tattoo on the top of her foot." Randy picked up some papers and stacked them at the corner of his desk, attempting to clear some space for his laptop. "As far as I know, Maris didn't have any tattoos. I'm sure the medical examiner's report will confirm it's not her." As he finished speaking, Randy's intercom buzzed.

"Detective?"

"Yes, Wanda."

"Linda Reeves is here. Says you're probably expecting her?"

"Yes, send her in."

"I'll let the two of you talk," Cynthia said, slowly backing out of Randy's office.

"Why don't you stay? I have a feeling you're going to end up being the one to go through this journal. I can't see Louise having the time for it. I'll check with her for sure, but you might as well stay."

Cynthia stepped back into Randy's office and took a seat on one of the chairs facing the mess he called a desk. She had learned a lot about fraud and several other financial crimes she hadn't known existed before working with Louise. The single member of the financial crimes department before Cynthia had started working with her, Louise had made sure to show Cynthia how to conduct a thorough investigation with proper documentation that would stand up in court.

Though Louise's training had been precise and enlightening, as she sat waiting for Linda to join them in Randy's office, Cynthia felt nervous about the potential fraud at Cooper Downs. When she had worked at D&A, they were always bidding on the audit work for Cooper Downs. The racetrack was owned by an international conglomerate, which meant potential for extra business if the audit went well. In turn, this meant a fraud investigation could be like stepping on a hornet's nest with bare feet.

7

It was almost 9 a.m. when Cynthia returned to her office. She'd left Randy and Linda discussing another case. Her cellphone buzzed in her bag. She'd hung it on the hook on the back of her office door on the way to Randy's office. She found the phone in her bag, looked at the call display, and smiled as she answered.

"Hi. I missed your voice this morning," she said, blushing as she realized she was getting used to Ben calling her every morning on his way to work at D&A.

"I'm sorry, babe. I couldn't sleep, so I went to work early to try and distract myself, and it worked a little too well. I got wrapped up in the audit file I'm working on." Ben sounded tired.

"It's okay. You don't have to call me every morning. You know that, right?"

"I know, but I like to check on you."

Cynthia admired Ben's chivalrous side. That part of him reminded her of Jason, the husband she'd lost two years ago in a car accident. She also admired how hard Ben worked. It was because of his help she'd been able to piece together the clues in the PPC fraud.

"I couldn't sleep either. I still can't believe someone felt their life was bad enough to jump off the roof of your building," Cynthia said.

"Crazy, right? But what if they weren't up there alone? What if they were pushed? There could be a murderer in my building."

The cynic in Cynthia had been thinking the same thing, but she hadn't mentioned it because she didn't want to alarm Ben. Relief flooded her body when she heard Ben had been thinking the same thing.

"I was wondering that too. I'm sure Randy will keep me in the loop. He mentioned he talked with you last night. He's pretty good about keeping in touch with witnesses." Cynthia had first-hand experience as a witness in the PPC case. She had been staring at the floor while she talked. When she looked up, she noticed Linda standing in the doorway smiling at her. She waved and held up her right pointer finger to let her know she'd just be a minute.

"Do you want to come over for dinner tonight?" she asked Ben. "Luke has been asking about you. I'm sure he'd love to see you."

"I'd love that. I'm not super excited about being alone in my apartment tonight. I hope you don't think less of me for of that. It's not very manly."

"Of course not. Let's eat around six. Come over any time before then. I should be home by five."

"I'll see you then. Have a good day, babe."

"You too." Cynthia put her cellphone back in her bag. Linda had made her way into Cynthia's office and was sitting in front of her desk.

"It's all yours," Linda said, placing the journal on Cynthia's desk. "I flagged the pages where Maris wrote her suspicions about Cooper Downs."

"Did you read it?" Cynthia asked as she grabbed the colourful notebook and flipped through it.

"Yes. Her life was in danger, Cyn. I would have disappeared too if I were her."

"You think she's hiding?" This wasn't Cynthia's first financial fraud case, and with Louise's help, she had seen the horrific lengths people would go to cover up their crimes. But this new information shocked her—Maris might be hiding because she feared for her life.

"I didn't read every single page," Linda continued, "but I read enough to know this is a good news story. I copied the pages I need. Randy wants you to let him know if you come across anything that might help him in the missing person's case.

He also said to tell you he'll have some notes for you from our meeting this morning once he's updated them."

"Okay, thanks. I hope we find her soon. It's been a couple of weeks hasn't it?" Cynthia asked Linda. She had an uncanny memory when it came to dates and timelines.

"Yes, but after reading that journal, it sounds to me like she doesn't want to be found." Linda tapped Cynthia's desk with her finger as she stood up and walked to the door.

"Was that Ben on the phone earlier? Got a hot date tonight?"

Of course, Linda already knew the answer, but Cynthia knew her friend couldn't resist teasing her.

"Very funny," Cynthia replied. "Just a quiet dinner at my place with Luke. Why don't you join us?"

"You know, I just might do that. It's been a while since I've seen your little munchkin. Later." Linda waved as she left Cynthia's office and continued down the hall.

8

The sticky notes Linda had left for Cynthia in Maris's journal were a rainbow mix of neon colours. Cynthia grabbed the first one, a bright yellow, and flipped to the page.

Tuesday, August 15, 2017

I'm not sure if what I saw today was correct. Vivian asked me to balance the racetrack ticket ledger. I found two identical ticket numbers. But the tickets are issued electronically. I don't understand how this is possible. I'll have to check again in the morning when my eyes are fresh. All this overtime is starting to get to me.

I'm 24 years old and have no life. All I do is work. And now I have to tell my boss that a staff member might be scamming her. The work part is fine, that's what I want anyway . . . I guess. It's nice they're paying for my designation and everything. I can't wait until I'm a CPA. Things will be so much better.

Cynthia smiled half-heartedly, remembering her own feelings about how her life would be so much better once this or that happened. How naïve she'd been at the beginning of her own career. She turned the page. There were at least four more neon sticky notes marking the pages Linda felt were important. She hoped the others contained more details. A couple of duplicate ticket numbers were definitely suspicious, but even Maris wasn't sure what she'd seen. That wasn't a lot to go on. Cynthia skipped to the beginning of the next journal entry.

Wednesday, August 16, 2017

What a shitty day. The tickets I thought were duplicates definitely are. Well, the ticket numbers in the ledger are the same anyway. I'll need to find the original tickets to know for sure. I tried to do that on my lunch break so I didn't get behind on my other work, but Paul wouldn't leave the office. He kept asking me personal questions, trying to start a conversation. I think he was hitting on me. I may have to be brutal with him.

Cynthia scanned the rest of the page looking for further information relating to the duplicate betting tickets then turned the page, accidentally grabbing two pages at the same time. Before turning back a page, something caught her eye.

Sexual harassment.

Cynthia glanced to the beginning of the journal entry.

Friday, August 18, 2017

TGIF!!! That's for damn sure! What a week. I'm so glad it's the weekend! I STILL haven't had a chance to look for those ticket stubs, but I need to do it soon. It's stressing me out worrying about how to tell Vivian. Then on top of that, I can't believe what Vivian asked me to do today.

Some big-time gamblers are coming to the track next week for the big Triple X race. Cooper Downs is having a big party for them. Vivian asked me to help her "entertain" them, whatever that means. That's all fine and good. I don't mind serving alcohol and snacks, but then she told me the men are pretty loose with their money, especially after a few drinks. If I wore something skimpy, I could probably make a whole week's wages that night UNDER THE TABLE. Under the table! I'm working for an accountant who actually suggested I accept money under the table. OMG! I told her I would help out, but I'd be wearing my usual office attire. She had the nerve to tell me if I wasn't there looking drop-dead gorgeous and showing lots of skin, she'd find someone else to do my job! And she wasn't just referring to the night of the party.

Ugh! This feels like sexual harassment. Fuck! I DO NOT need this right now. But I really need the money. I never expected a place like Cooper Downs operated like this. Guess I'll be shopping for a skimpy party dress or looking for another job this weekend. All right, I'm off to vomit and watch some Netflix. I can't believe this . . .

The thought of Cooper Downs treating their employees like that made Cynthia wonder what else they were capable of. She didn't know much about the horse-racing industry, but everyone knew it wasn't kosher to suggest their employees dress skimpy or accept cash under the table. Maybe there was more fraud at Cooper Downs than she'd bargained for. She was certainly willing to find out. It was time to get this investigation started.

"Knock, knock," Randy said as he poked his head into Cynthia's office. Cynthia looked up from the journal, her heart beating faster than usual. "You all right handling the Cooper Downs fraud case on your own?"

"On my own? I'm not sure what you mean?"

"I just talked to Louise. She thinks you're ready to handle this on your own."

"I've been reading Maris's journal, and this might be beyond me. There are things happening at Cooper Downs—more than just financial fraud—sexual harassment and violations of employee labour standards. This isn't my area of expertise." Cynthia's excitement about a new case had turned to fear about what else she might find in connection with Cooper Downs.

"It's time you start taking cases on your own. Don't worry, you can handle it." Randy sounded like he was convinced.

"Really?" Weren't there certain rules that needed to be followed? "But, I'm not a Certified Fraud Examiner yet." As soon as the words left her mouth, she realized how lame she sounded.

"You know as well as I do that's just a formality. It's the on-the-job experience that's important, and Louise is the best. I'm sure she's already taught you everything you need to know." Randy had a point. Cynthia glanced to the white binder she kept on her bookshelf to her right. Her fraud investigation procedures bible. It was full of all kinds of notes she'd taken in the last three months.

"And," Randy continued, "I've got more good news for you." Cynthia didn't like the way Randy stressed the word "good". Thick sarcasm hung in the air like the smell of dirty socks. "I'm going to need your help finding this woman. Anything in the journal that can help that part of the case, I need to know."

Sensing she was fighting a losing battle, Cynthia agreed. "Of course. But are you sure? What if I miss something? This goes beyond numbers. You're talking about saving a person's life now."

"Come on, Cynthia. You're thorough. I've seen your eye for detail, and you've got great gut instincts. You're not going to miss anything." Randy stepped further into Cynthia's office. "Besides, you don't have a choice. Louise just got called to Toronto to help with a case there."

"What?" Cynthia interrupted. "No way. I can't handle this one on my own. Maybe if it was a simple fraud case, but there's way more going on at Cooper Downs than that."

"There's nobody else, Cynthia. I need your help."

With pursed lips, Cynthia shook her head, glanced down at the journal, and shifted focus. "What's Louise doing in Toronto, anyway?"

"The Toronto police need help with some German financial records. Louise is fluent. You know you can call her any time you have questions, right?"

"I'm not worried about that. It's finding Maris Kane I'm worried about."

"You'll just be feeding me information. I'll be doing the heavy lifting. Don't worry about it."

9

After work, when she should have been relaxing with her best friend and son, Cynthia was still stressing about the Cooper Downs case.

"You're worrying for nothing, Cyn. You'll be fine." Linda was excited Detective Bain had asked Cynthia to help him find Maris Kane.

"But I'm a numbers person!"

The best friends sat at Cynthia's dining room table enjoying some pinot grigio and watching Luke colour while Cynthia kept an eye on the stir-fry simmering on the stove.

"Besides, Detective Bain wouldn't have asked for your help if he didn't think you could handle it. Why don't we go poke around the casino tomorrow?" Linda was itching to get some answers, not just for the general public, but especially for Maris's mother.

"Are you *nuts*?! I don't have permission to investigate. I'm just supposed to report to Randy. Tell him what I find in the journal."

"Come on. Don't you have permission to investigate the fraud?" Linda sure was convincing when she wanted her way. "It will ease your mind to see what you're getting into. Besides, I *am* an investigator. That's what I do every time I follow a story. Help me find Maris and nail Cooper Downs to the wall." Linda's fiery passion for her work was shining brightly. Cynthia loved that about her friend.

"I don't know. These guys are big. They're part of an international, publicly traded company. I don't—"

"That's exactly why we need to take them down. They can't get away with this shit." Linda pounded her fist on the table and Luke looked up from his colouring.

"Ha, ha! Auntie Linda said a bad word," Luke laughed, and Linda smiled at him while covering her potty mouth. Cynthia shot Linda a warning glance then leaned close to her as she got up to check the stir-fry.

"I forgot just how large your lady balls are," Cynthia whispered, so Luke couldn't hear. Linda gently backhanded Cynthia on the arm and smirked.

"Okay, buddy," Cynthia said to Luke. "It's time to put your colouring away. Dinner's ready." Luke frowned a little but started cleaning up with Linda's help.

"Isn't Ben coming?" Linda asked.

"He's supposed to be. I told him we were eating at 6:00, and it's already 6:15. He probably got stuck at work." Cynthia set some plates and cutlery down on the table, and Linda distributed them to the appropriate places.

"This one's for me, right?" Linda said, tapping Luke with a Spider-Man cup.

Luke laughed and said, "No, that's mine, silly."

***

As the trio finished their dinner, Cynthia saw a taxi pull into her driveway. She watched out the window while Ben stumbled out of the cab. It was clear he had been drinking. A lot. Cynthia went outside to head him off at the pass. She signalled to the driver for him to stay.

"Hey, Cyn. I'm sorry I missed dinner. I brought some wine." Ben held up a bottle in a brown paper bag as he swayed from side to side.

"I don't think you need any more wine." Cynthia took the bottle from Ben.

"I'm sorry. Ryan and I went for drinks after work."

"Clearly. Why don't you go home and sober up?"

"Can't I stay here tonight?"

"No way. I don't want to explain to Luke why you're acting so strange."

"Please. I can't stay at my apartment. I can't stop thinking about what happened last night." Ben tried to grab Cynthia's free hand. She pulled away even though she knew exactly how he felt. Part of her wanted to comfort him, but most of her was pissed he missed dinner without so much as a phone call.

"I'm sure Ryan will let you crash on his couch." Cynthia turned her back on Ben before she changed her mind and headed back inside where Luke and Linda had cleaned up dinner and were looking at a book.

Luke looked up at Cynthia. "Mommy, why don't you want to work with Auntie Linda?"

Cynthia turned to Linda, still angry from her conversation with Ben. "Did you put him up to this?" Her tone was a little sharper than she'd intended.

"Hey, now. I don't know what just happened out there, but Luke and I have better things to talk about than you." Linda widened her eyes and cocked her head to the side. "I think it'd be pretty fun teaming up to find this woman."

"You would think that," Cynthia said. Linda seemed to have an abnormal attraction to danger. It made her an exceptional reporter. "You know what, maybe a little recon work at the casino will help me get a jump on things." Cynthia paused, warming to the idea of going to the casino with Linda. "Randy better not find out about this. Dammit!"

"It doesn't matter if he does. As an investigative reporter, I have every right to be researching this story. It's not like you're going to be keeping anything from him anyway. He asked you to tell him what you find out." Cynthia nodded in agreement. He did say he needed her help, and she liked the idea of scoping out the casino before officially starting to investigate the fraud allegations; it would be a chance to get her bearings.

"You want to talk about what Ben's up to?"

"Let's just say I knew it was a bad idea to date a younger man." She lowered her gaze and took a slow breath. Ben was good to her. "Forget I said that. I think he's just having a tough time with what happened last night. Maybe Randy will have some news I can pass along to him tomorrow."

10

The next morning, work wasn't helping keep Cynthia's mind off Ben. She hadn't heard from him all day and it bothered her. She wanted to see how he was doing, but she was stubborn and still angry, and she was hoping to be a little more cool-headed the next time she talked to him.

Maris's journal sat in front of Cynthia. It was proving to be a gold mine of evidence against Cooper Downs. Sexual harassment, fraud, and employee labour code violations were the big ones on the list. But Linda was going to have her work cut out for her if she wanted to "nail Cooper Downs to the wall," as she put it. From what Cynthia could tell, all Maris's complaints stemmed from one person—her boss, Vivian Lennings. After reading most of Maris's journal, Cynthia was confident she could summarize the important parts Detective Bain needed for his missing person's case and document the evidence regarding the fake winning tickets. She felt more connected to Maris and was determined to figure out what had happened to her. She marched down the hall to Randy's office. It was a large office, but the filing cabinets along the walls on either side of his desk made it seem small. Were the cabinets stuffed so full of paper there wasn't any more room? Is that why he left so much paper on his desk? And what about all the talk around the office about going paperless? Clearly, Randy hadn't embraced that yet.

Randy was on the phone, shuffling through papers while he talked as usual. He looked up and waved Cynthia in. "Yes, Mrs. Kane, I assure you we are investigating all possible leads. I hate to say this, but if your daughter doesn't want to be found, there's not much anyone can do."

Cynthia cringed at the sound of this. She could only imagine what Mrs. Kane was saying in response to the idea her daughter didn't want to be found. Randy hadn't been very professional. The lack of news must be killing her. Randy uttered some routine pleasantries then hung up.

"Have a seat, Cynthia. That was Amarillis Kane's mother, and I don't want to hear any more about why you shouldn't be helping me find her." Cynthia didn't have a chance to answer before Randy added, "I still need your help."

"About that . . ." Cynthia held up Maris's journal.

"I told you yesterday, you're the best person to help with this."

"It's not that. I've read both the journal and a letter Maris wrote to her mom. She makes some serious allegations against Cooper Downs besides the financial fraud—sexual harassment, employee labour code violations."

"Well, sexual harassment falls under the labour code, and without Maris around to make a statement, there's not much we can do about it at this point."

"It looks like her boss, and maybe a guy named Paul, were giving her the most trouble."

"I'm glad to see you've changed your mind about being involved in this. I don't have to remind you about talking to the press, right?"

"No, but if it wasn't for Linda, we wouldn't even have this journal." Her words cut through the air. Why did he have to bring up Linda? "What you said to Mrs. Kane might be true," Cynthia said, taking a letter Maris had written to her mom out of the journal. "Maris left this letter for her mom when she disappeared. She went into hiding because she feared for her life. She believed she was being followed, and her journal documents a number of threats to her life."

"Jesus." Randy shook his head. "If she doesn't want to be found, I'm not sure how we're going to build a case against Cooper Downs if there really were fraudulent winnings as Maris suggests in her journal. See why I need your help on this?"

"Well, the financial fraud will speak for itself. But I'll need access to Cooper Downs's network to find the evidence. I'll check with Wade in legal and see if he thinks there's enough evidence in the journal to warrant a subpoena. As for the other issues, Maris seems to blame her boss, Vivian Lennings."

"That doesn't surprise me." Randy's tone was cold as he glanced in Cynthia's direction.

"You know her?" Cynthia asked.

"Our paths have crossed a time or two. I interviewed her when Maris first went missing." Randy leaned back in his chair. "Let's just say those accusations don't surprise me, but I would still prefer to find Maris before I press any charges. Does Maris say who was threatening her?"

"Not directly, but she thought Paul and two other men were following her."

"Hmmm, okay. Talk to Wade and get going on your plan for the financial fraud investigation."

"Will do. Any news on the Jane Doe from Ben's building?" Cynthia stood and walked towards the hallway.

"Yes and no. I got the ME's report from Troy, and it confirmed the body wasn't Maris, but we still don't know who she was. Still Jane Doe unless we find evidence otherwise. I'll let you know if I get any leads."

"Thanks," Cynthia said. She was thankful there was still hope for finding Maris, but she wished she had some news she could pass on to Ben to give him some closure.

11

Randy Bain was not a liar, and he hated that he was lying to Cynthia now, but he had no choice. Vivian had his nuts in a vise, and she was squeezing them. Hard. He wasn't sure how he was going to get out of this godforsaken situation he'd gotten himself into, but he was a fighter, and he always tried to make things right. It's why he'd become a cop.

The usual grey cityscape had dimmed somewhat, but it wasn't quite dark yet when Randy pulled into his driveway. He could have sworn he'd turned off all the lights when he left this morning, but now his modest home was lit from within. There was no bark from Boo either as he fiddled with his key in the lock. Odd.

When he opened the door, no sloppy-tongued, furry friend greeted him at the door.

"Boo? Where you at, boy?"

He heard the Aerosmith CD he'd been listening to earlier wafting out from the back bedroom. His bedroom. For a moment he hoped it was Kat, the woman he'd loved years ago who'd come barging back into his life via the PPC case he'd worked months ago. But his instincts told him otherwise. He drew his service weapon and crept down the hall. He paused beside the bedroom door, back pressed against the wall.

"Hello, Detective." It was Vivian. Part of him wanted to scare her with his Glock 17 pistol, but the rest of him knew a woman like Vivian Lennings didn't shy from danger. He tucked his Glock back in its holster and moved to the doorway. Vivian was wearing a sparkly, floor-length party dress that emphasized her ample cleavage. She'd taken her shoes off and was sprawled out on Randy's neatly made bed.

"I thought we were meeting at the casino?"

Vivian paused the CD. "Just wanted to make sure you weren't getting cold feet." She got up to face Randy. Even without her heels, she stood at least an inch taller.

Randy's gaze landed on Boo, who was asleep in the corner, completely oblivious to Randy's presence. "What the hell did you do to my dog?" He rushed to Boomer and stroked his ears.

"Relax. He's fine. I just gave him an extra special treat."

"Did you drug my dog?"

"Like I said, I need a little insurance you're going to hold up your end of the bargain."

"I said I was in and I'm in, but this is more than insurance Vivian. This feels like a threat."

"Call it what you want, Detective. He'll be fine."

"Jesus Christ, you better hope so." Randy put his hand on Boo's chest as the dog took a big breath and one of his front paws twitched. He'd never seen him so apathetic. It made him sick to his stomach.

"I told you, he's fine. Come on, this deal is about us helping each other. What would I have to gain by killing your dog?" Vivian extended a hand to help Randy up from the floor. He glared at her but took her hand anyway. "I'll see you tonight, Detective. And don't be late."

"You'll see me tonight if I think my dog can survive being alone."

"I'll see you tonight, or the deal's off." Vivian put on her heels and Randy suddenly felt like a much smaller man than he was. "Besides," Vivian continued, "I'll have your first instalment ready." She stepped close enough that Randy could smell her perfume. Vanilla and jasmine. He hated to admit he liked it. She lightly traced his arm with her manicured fingers, gave his bicep a squeeze, and left his room.

Randy followed her down the hall and out the front door. He watched her walk to the end of the street in her fancy dress and heels where she disappeared down a side street. Where had she come from, and exactly how far did she expect to get in those shoes?

The hint of a plan formed in his mind. Maybe there was a way he could keep his deal with Vivian and do his job as an honest cop after all. He hoped he hadn't just blown his chance. He pulled his phone out of his back pocket and dialed Kat. As a private investigator in Denver, Colorado, she was the perfect person to bounce ideas off. Plus, he needed to hear her voice.

12

When Cynthia arrived at the back entry of her rancher after work, she was surprised to see Linda's white Toyota Tercel hatchback parked in her driveway next to Mom's car. Linda must have seen her arrive. She'd barely gotten out of her car and Linda already had the back door open for her. Linda was abuzz with plans.

"Cyn, I'm taking you out!" Linda looked gorgeous, as usual, in a simple red dress and heels.

"Oh, really?" Cynthia wasn't convinced.

"I already checked with Gayle and she's fine with cooking Luke dinner and watching him until we get back."

"Is that so?" Cynthia looked at Mom who shrugged her shoulders.

"Luke and I will be fine. Your dad's coming over to join us. You girls go have some fun."

"Well, the two of you make it hard to argue."

"Yes," Linda said as she did a fist pump in the air while looking at Luke, who laughed and jumped up and down.

"You're incorrigible," Cynthia said, shaking her head.

"So where are we going? Is what I'm wearing okay?" She looked down at her dark dress pants and light grey blouse then back at her fancy-looking friend. "On second thought, give me a sec to change and put on some lipstick."

In ten minutes, Cynthia was dressed in a simple black knee-length dress and had applied a fresh coat of rose-tinted lip gloss that complimented her olive complexion and dark hair. Since Linda was the one with the master plan, she drove and informed Cynthia they were going for dinner at the casino with the ulterior motive of scoping the place out. Cynthia wasn't convinced a dinner out was going to help with either the fraud investigation or the disappearance of Maris Kane, but knowing how Linda was when she got an idea, she went along.

The pair arrived at the Cooper Downs casino lounge twenty minutes later looking like they were ready to take on the world. It wasn't quite 5:30 p.m., and because it was mid-week, there were plenty of tables to choose from. Cynthia hadn't been in a casino in years and revelled in the magic of it all—the flashing lights, the music, and the ringing of the slot machines. Minors were allowed in the restaurant, so it was separated from the slot machines and card tables by a half-wall. Patrons on either side could see into the other.

Cynthia and Linda were seated near the half-wall separating the restaurant from the casino. They each ordered white wine that arrived in chilled glasses.

"Fancy," Cynthia said to Linda as they opened their menus. "Don't think for one second I believe you came up with this little plan spur of the moment."

"You know I love my research, and when I'm chasing a story, I can never get enough. I wanted to show you how I research in the field."

"Oh please, I'm fine researching from behind my desk. But I'll play along for now. Besides, I've heard this place has great Greek food." Cynthia glanced past her friend and into the gambling area. Against the far wall were two large screens—one to view the live horse races and one for video horse racing. Cynthia noticed a familiar face sitting at the blackjack table.

"Who's that with Detective Bain? I didn't know he had a girlfriend."

Linda shook her head and said, "Oh that's not his girlfriend. That's Vivian Lennings. They do look awfully cozy though."

"Lennings? Oh, Maris's boss. Right?" Cynthia remembered the unflattering things she'd read about Vivian in Maris's journal.

"Vivian's son works at Cooper Downs too," Linda said.

"Isn't that a little weird?"

"Not really. Cooper Downs has a great referral program where employees get cash bonuses for referring successful employment applicants. Vivian is the controller here, and her son works security."

"Sounds like you've done a lot of research already."

"Maris has been missing for two weeks already," Linda said, closing her menu. "S-CAL's received a number of tips I've followed up on personally."

The waitress appeared, and the two friends ordered another round of wine and their meals—souvlaki for Linda and Greek ribs for Cynthia.

"I hope Randy's not questioning her about the gambling fraud before I've had a chance to look at the accounting records. She could change anything she wanted. Maybe I should go over there?" Cynthia said, standing.

"You're not going anywhere. Detective Bain's a professional. He wouldn't do anything like that," Linda scolded her friend as the waitress left two full glasses of wine on the table to accompany the almost empty glasses already there. "Besides, looks like you've got bigger problems," she said gesturing towards the restaurant entrance.

Cynthia sat back down and turned to see what Linda was talking about. As she craned her head around to look behind her, Cynthia saw Ben storming into the restaurant. Even from where she sat, his green eyes seemed to take on an amber hue.

"This ought to be interesting," she said, just loud enough so Linda could hear.

"I'll give you two some time," Linda said, standing.

"No. Stay," Cynthia said, grabbing her friend's hand. Cynthia could almost feel the floor shaking as Ben stomped over to their table. In the three months she and Ben had been dating, she couldn't remember ever having seen him angry. She was afraid to look him in the eyes but did anyway.

"Hi." The word barely came out of her mouth. "What's going on?"

"I'll be the one asking the questions." Ben crossed his arms over his chest. "So, you're the only one who's allowed to have any fun in this relationship?" Ben gestured at the wine glasses on the table.

"It's not what you think." Cynthia tried to defend herself. What had gotten into him? This wasn't like him at all.

"Oh, really? It looks like you and Linda are having a fun time drinking some wine. Not unlike what Ryan and I did last night. This feels like a double standard, Cynthia."

"And that's my cue." Linda stood and faced Ben. "Why don't you take my seat?"

"I'm not staying." Ben turned on his heels and headed for the door.

"Shit," Cynthia said under her breath, glancing at Linda and getting up to follow Ben. "Ben, wait," she called after him, but he didn't stop until they had passed through the lobby doors leading out to the parking lot. He turned around and Cynthia could see his anger had turned to something else. There was more going on with him.

"You know what? I . . . I need some time to think about things. I'm not sure this relationship is going in the direction I want it to. Don't call me for a while." He tripped over the curb as he scurried away.

"But, Ben," Cynthia called after him, but he was already halfway to his car. Tears threatened Cynthia's eyes as she headed back into the restaurant, stunned by what had just happened. Maybe Linda would have some insights into Ben's strange behaviour. She was better at dealing with men than Cynthia, almost like she spoke their secret language.

But when she got back to the table, Linda wasn't there. Their meals had arrived, and it was clear Linda hadn't waited to start on her souvlaki, but where was she now? Cynthia wasn't hungry anymore. She picked up her wine and took a sip. She grimaced—it hadn't tasted so bitter before.

Ten minutes passed, and Linda still hadn't returned to the table. That wasn't like her. Cynthia looked around the restaurant, hoping to see her friend appear from behind one of the slot machines or from down the corridor that led to the ladies' room. She looked over to where Detective Bain had been sitting with Vivian Lennings. Their chairs were both empty. When the waitress returned to ask how the food was, Cynthia asked if she had seen her friend. The waitress told her Linda had gone in the direction of the bathroom about half an hour ago.

"Thank you," Cynthia said, standing to go check on Linda. The washroom was deserted when Cynthia got there. There was nobody around to ask if they'd seen Linda. When Cynthia returned from the bathroom, she found a note at her table. "Leave now."

Not wanting to attract attention, she quickly shoved the note into her coat pocket then looked around for a clue as to who could have left it. The other restaurant patrons were enjoying their dinners, minding their own business. Cynthia approached the waitress at the bar on her way out. "Did you see anyone at my table while I was gone?" she asked.

"Just your friend." Cynthia must have looked confused because the waitress added, "The one you arrived with."

"Okay, thank you." Cynthia gave the waitress enough cash to cover the meal and a generous tip. What the hell? Had she really come back to the table while Cynthia was in the washroom?

She looked at the note again. The writing definitely wasn't Linda's. Cynthia quickened her pace, hoping Linda had gone to get something from her car. As she weaved through the other cars in the lot, she felt herself losing her breath. Why did Linda always have to park so far away from the entrance?

Finally, she arrived at Linda's hatchback. The driver's door was open. The sense of relief Cynthia felt disappeared when she realized Linda was nowhere to be found.

Cynthia pulled her cellphone out of her pocket and dialed Detective Bain. It went straight to voicemail, so she left a message. "Something's happened to Linda. We're at the casino." Distracted by the dark and wet appearance of the pavement under the open car door, Cynthia bent down and touched the pavement. Blood covered her fingers. She forgot all about the message she was leaving for Detective Bain, hung up, and called 911.

"Come on, Linda, where are you?" Cynthia whispered under her breath as all kinds of vicious scenarios flooded her mind.

13

Kelly White, head groomer at the Cooper Downs stables, felt her
heart racing as her dark-coloured, tattered pickup truck barely
rolled to a stop in front of the emergency entrance to the Dan
Gross Centre. She saw people leaving the hospital. Her nerves
taking over, she reached over the limp body in the passenger seat,
opened the door, and shoved her out of the vehicle.

"Oh, God," she said out loud as she watched the body flop to
the ground. "I'm so sorry it has to be this way."

She yanked the door shut and squealed the tires to get back
on the road. She'd taken precautions to drive to the farthest
hospital from the casino, hoping nobody would think to make
a note of her licence plate. There were many beat-up Ford
F-150s in the city.

A man and woman ran over to the body. "Help! Somebody
help! She's not breathing!" The man ran into the hospital to get
someone who knew what they were doing while the woman
stayed with the victim. When he returned, he was accompanied
by two nurses with a gurney. One of the nurses lowered the
stretcher to ground level while the other one checked the body
for vital signs.

"I've got a pulse," she said. Together the two nurses carefully
put the woman on the gurney and headed towards the emergency
entrance. An ER doctor met them at the doorway.

"Did anybody call the police?" he asked. The woman who
had yelled for help took her cellphone out of her purse and
dialed 911.

"It's ringing," she said as she held the phone to her ear.

Inside the emergency room, the nurses and doctors were busy

working on the woman, hooking up monitors and determining how best to help her. Once the woman was stable and the sense of urgency had died down, one of the nurses paused and took a good look at her face.

"Holy shit. It's Linda Reeves from the news," she said. Another nurse looked up from what she was doing.

"You're right. She's from S-CAL. I just saw her live on the news earlier today. She must have riled someone's feathers to be dumped outside like that."

***

Detective Bain was on his way back to the station from the casino when he heard the scanner buzz about the drop off at the hospital. Although he was off duty, he decided to go to the Dan Gross Centre himself because it was on the way to the station. At the hospital, several witnesses told Detective Bain about the dark-coloured pickup truck, black or navy blue, probably a 1990s model, they'd said. He got several numbers from the licence plate but none of them were complete, and none of the witnesses had noted any of the same numbers. All they could agree on was the plate was from Alberta.

When he asked about the condition of the victim, Detective Bain was told she was still unconscious, and hospital staff recognized her as Linda Reeves from the news channel S-CAL. She'd suffered a life-threatening blow to the back of the head doctors were currently tending to. A squad car arrived while Detective Bain was collecting statements, and officers started surveying the roped-off area for evidence. As Detective Bain walked to the scene where Linda had been tossed out of the truck to check in with his officers, he dialed his voicemail and listened to the message from Cynthia.

"Any leads?" he asked, after listening to Cynthia's message and tucking his cell in his back pocket.

"Nothing yet, Detective," replied Warren Scott, the officer

closest to him.

"I want you to make this case a priority, Warren."

"You got it."

Detective Bain headed back to the emergency room, dialing Cynthia's number as he walked.

***

Cynthia didn't understand how Linda could disappear in such a short time. Nausea crept in. Her mind raced with thoughts about what had happened to cause so much bleeding. It was Linda's blood, she was certain of that.

She'd called 911, and the ambulance had come and gone, but without a victim to assess, there was nothing they could do. A squad car had come and gone too, and an officer she didn't recognize took some photos and collected evidence. They'd found Linda's car keys under her car and suspected they'd fallen there when she was hurt.

The ring of her cellphone from inside her pocket made Cynthia jump, and she recognized the ringtone as the one she'd assigned to Randy's number.

"Randy?" she answered.

"Hi, Cynthia. I've got some bad news."

"It's Linda, isn't it?"

"Yeah. She's at the Don Gross Centre. I won't know exactly what happened until I can talk to her, and I'm not sure when that will be. I'm going to wait here until I know."

"I'm on my way." Cynthia hung up without saying goodbye and jumped in Linda's car, thankful the officer had left the keys with her.

14

The tea in Cynthia's travel mug was as cool as dirty dish water by the time she arrived at the office the next morning. She'd been in and out of sleep while waiting at the hospital for Linda to wake up. But she never did open her eyes. The doctors had stitched her up, but she remained unconscious with no indication of when her status might change, so Cynthia had stayed until an orderly had roused her in the waiting room. Linda's parents were vacationing in Mexico, and Cynthia had been able to notify them. They would be on the next available flight to Calgary.

Mom and Dad had stayed at Cynthia's overnight with Luke. They were still there now. She was lucky her son could spend lots of time with his grandparents while she worked, but she looked forward to not having to rely on her parents so much when he went to preschool. They had helped her so much since Jason had died. She knew they felt partially responsible for his death, even though it had been an accident caused by icy winter roads.

Cynthia parked her red Ford Focus in the police station's staff parking lot while she covered her mouth and let it stretch into a big yawn. She rubbed her eyes, hoping the scratchy feeling would disappear soon so she could plan how she was going to investigate the duplicate winning tickets at Cooper Downs. Maris had mentioned three separate instances in her journal. Cynthia had to stay open to the possibility there might be more than one perpetrator.

She put her keys in her coat pocket and felt a piece of paper she didn't remember being there. It was the mysterious note from last night. She took it out to have another look. The printing was neat and done using a marker. Maybe a Sharpie?

As she wandered down the hall to Randy's office, she wished she hadn't shoved it in her pocket so carelessly, potentially ruining any evidence of who'd written it.

"Morning," she said as she knocked on Randy's half-open door.

"You know you don't need to knock, right?" Randy seemed chipper considering he had been at the hospital most of the night with Cynthia. Victims always remembered the best details closest to the time the crime was committed he'd told her. He hadn't wanted to miss his chance to question Linda the instant she woke up.

"This was at my table last night when I got back from looking for Linda." Cynthia handed the piece of paper to Randy. "I'm sorry I didn't mention it last night. It was in my pocket the whole time."

"That's understandable. You were worried about your friend. I'll get this to evidence. See if it holds any clues for us."

Cynthia nodded and turned to head back to her office. It was odd Wade in legal hadn't gotten back to her about whether they had enough evidence to issue a subpoena. She was itching to get out to Cooper Downs and get to the bottom of those fake tickets. She picked up the phone on her desk and dialed Wade.

In Cynthia's mind, Wade was some sort of child genius. He barely looked old enough to attend university, let alone have a law degree already. Not only was he incredibly intelligent, but he was extremely efficient as well, which made it even stranger she hadn't heard back from him yesterday.

Wade answered with his usual businesslike greeting, "Wade Martin."

"Hi, Wade. It's Cynthia Webber. Did you have a chance to look at my subpoena request for Cooper Downs?"

"Absolutely. You didn't get it? I issued the subpoena within the hour I received your request. There's definitely enough evidence in that journal to warrant an investigation."

"It must have gotten lost at reception somewhere. That happens sometimes with everything coming and going around here," Cynthia said. Strange for a subpoena to be missing. They were usually given top priority.

"Detective Bain was here yesterday on another matter," said Wade. "I gave it directly to him." Wade was sounding a little defensive. "I'll get one of our administrators to fax you another copy right away."

"Thank you. I'll head to the fax machine and wait for it."

Cynthia heard a click in her ear as Wade hung up without bothering to say goodbye.

15

Kelly and Paul met in the parking lot behind the stables at Cooper Downs. Paul had just arrived for his shift, and Kelly had returned to the parking lot to get the work gloves she'd forgotten in her vehicle when she'd arrived earlier that morning.

"I told you before, it's impossible. If they really are unclaimed tickets, there's no way they can be traced," Kelly said, grabbing her gloves out of her Ford F-150. She took a deep breath before turning to face Paul and added, "There was no reason for you to hurt that reporter."

"What do you mean?" Paul asked, pulling a bag out of his newer-model Jeep.

"I saw you in the parking lot last night. I saw you smash her head into her car door."

"How could you? I made sure nobody was around, and I shielded her from the cameras." Paul looked over his shoulder, checking to make sure no one else was around.

"I can't help you with those tickets if people are going to get hurt," Kelly said.

"Well, fuck!" Paul threw up his arms as he tossed his duffle bag on the hood of his Jeep. "She's always sticking her nose where it doesn't belong." He unzipped his bag and pulled out his security vest and hat. "I was just letting her know it's time for her to find a new story," he said, putting on his uniform.

"You don't even know she was checking into us . . ." Kelly paused, watching her words. Clearly Paul was a loose cannon. Memories of what he'd done to her years ago suddenly came flooding back. She started to walk away from her truck, but Paul stepped in front of her and put his hand on the hood of her truck, blocking her path.

He gritted his teeth before saying, "But this whole scam doesn't work without you." His glare seared into her eyes, causing her confidence to falter. She thought about her family and the hell Paul had put her through in school. How could it be she was letting him bully her again? She felt disgusted.

"Exactly," she said, her voice softer than before. She took a breath and averted her eyes from Paul's. She felt a bit of courage return. "I won't have anybody gettin' hurt over this. Rippin' off the track is bad enough—"

"I'll turn you in." He practically spat the words at her as he leaned in too close for comfort. Kelly stepped back.

"That won't matter much if I turn myself in." She found her nerve and met Paul's glare. "If you keep hurting people, that's exactly what I'll do." Kelly turned and went around the back end of her truck so she could get to the stables and back to work. Thankfully, Paul stayed where he was. Her face felt hot and her eyes burned. She blinked back tears as she stomped along the grassy earth separating the parking lot from the stables.

"Whatever," Paul said under his breath. He flipped the bird at Kelly's backside and headed off in the opposite direction, across the parking lot to the casino.

16

As she stood at the reception area of the police station, Cynthia reviewed the subpoena from Wade a little quicker than she normally would have and popped it in the laptop bag slung over her shoulder. She was eager to get out to Cooper Downs and start investigating.

"I'm heading out to Cooper Downs, Wanda," she said to the receptionist as she walked by Wanda's desk and straight for the main entry of the building. "I may not be back today. Depends how everything goes out there."

Wanda waved but otherwise remained glued to her computer screen. Cynthia wondered if what she'd said had even registered. They had her cell if they needed to track her down.

The drive north of the city limits where Cooper Downs was located took about thirty minutes. Cynthia used the time to think about Linda and Ben. She wanted to call Ben and tell him what had happened to Linda, but he'd told her not to call. She thought about Linda and her investigative skills. Where would she look to find out more about Maris's disappearance? While Cynthia had a solid plan for the fraud investigation, the missing person's case was way out of her league. She hoped some ideas would come to her as she snooped around the grounds of Cooper Downs.

Cynthia pulled into the parking lot at the front of the casino, trying not to think about the pool of Linda's blood that had been spilled a few parking spaces behind her. It would be gone by now anyway. Feeling a little uneasy about the note she'd received last night and thinking like an investigator might, Cynthia decided to leave her sunglasses on while she walked the grounds. Luckily, the sun was shining. She'd have no problem blending in.

The racetrack was almost directly behind the casino, and the horse stables were to the left. The best route to the racetrack was through the restaurant and casino where she'd been not even twenty-four hours ago.

She briskly made her way through the casino, glancing at the racing monitors long enough to know there weren't any live races today. As she exited in the direction of the track, she was shocked to find there weren't any grandstands. Spectators could watch from inside on the monitors or at ground level at the edge of the track. They must pack in like sardines on race day, with the spectators in the back barely being able to see. Surely they had a portable grandstand they pulled out for race days.

As she turned around, Cynthia nearly ran right into a tall security guard making his rounds. Due to their height difference, she was level with the name "Paul" embroidered on the chest pocket of his vest. Was he Vivian's son, the Paul Maris had written about in her journal?

"Excuse me, Ma'am," he said, stepping to the side, narrowly missing a collision with Cynthia. His overly formal politeness and the fact she couldn't see his eyes through his mirrored sunglasses unnerved Cynthia. She collected herself as Paul continued in his original direction.

She looked up at the casino. The rear entrance now faced her. The second level caught her attention. That must be where Maris had worked. There didn't seem to be any other logical place for administration offices. A patio restaurant and observation deck were located on the right-hand side of the second level, and she wondered how to get there. At least some of the patrons would have a good view of the races.

As she walked towards the back entry to the main building, Cynthia spotted an opening with some stairs she assumed led to the second floor and hastened her pace.

17

From the second-floor restaurant patio, Cynthia had a much better view of the racetrack. She saw Paul chatting with a burly woman standing near the starting gates. The woman could easily take him in a fight even though she was a bit shorter. Cynthia wished she had binoculars so she could see their expressions more clearly. It didn't seem like a friendly chat, and Cynthia wondered if the grounds were part of Paul's regular patrol area. The woman tossed her arms in the air as if to tell Paul to get lost. He gestured back to her, walking backwards ten steps or so before he turned and stomped back towards the casino.

The hair on the back of Cynthia's neck bristled. Innocent until proven guilty, she reminded herself, but she did not like the vibe this Paul guy was giving off. Maybe Maris was right about him being the one who'd been following her. Maris had written about two other men, but she hadn't used names or given any descriptions other than she thought they were friends of Paul's.

Was he the one who'd left the note last night? She'd have to keep her eye on him, and she shuddered at the thought of having to interview him. Hopefully Randy had already taken care of that.

Across from the entrance of the upper-level restaurant was a hallway labelled, "Administration". This must be where she needed to go to check Maris's computer. She proceeded down the hall that opened into a small reception area. Seated there was a young woman who looked to be in her early twenties. She looked up at Cynthia.

"Can I help you?" she asked.

"Yes, I'm looking for Vivian Lennings."

"Is she expecting you?"

"No, I'm Cynthia Webber. From the police department."

"I'm sorry, Vivian doesn't take unannounced appointments."

Well, la-dee-dah, thought Cynthia.

"I have a subpoena here. I'd like to talk with Vivian first, but if that's not possible, I guess I'll just take what I need."

"Oh. She's not going to like that." The receptionist's tone was protective. She picked up the phone and pressed a button. "Hi. Is Vivian back there?" Her eyes never strayed from Cynthia's. "All right. Thanks."

"Vivian's not in her office. I'll have her paged. Is there anything else I can do for you?"

Without saying anything, Cynthia showed the receptionist the court order. The receptionist looked as though she'd swallowed her tongue, and she sat a little straighter and taller.

"Yes," Cynthia said. "Were you friends with Maris Kane?" She seemed about the same age as Maris.

"Not really. I mean, we were friendly, but we didn't hang out or anything like that."

"Okay. And who's covering her work now that she's missing?"

"That would be the other bookkeeper. She's super swamped now." The receptionist made a sympathetic face. "Someone already interviewed all of us about Maris's disappearance. What do you need to discuss with Vivian?"

"I'm sorry, it's official police business," Cynthia replied. Any explanation about the fraud could give employees time to cover it up.

"Can you show me Maris's desk?" Cynthia asked.

"Sure. It's over here." The receptionist led Cynthia past her desk into a bullpen where three separate desks with computer stations were set up.

"This is Sherie." The receptionist gestured to a middle-aged woman, hard at work at her desk. She wore thick-rimmed glasses, and her brown hair revealed a lot of grey.

"One second," Sherie said, not glancing up from the paperwork in front of her or taking her hand off her adding machine. She furiously finished her row of adding, totalled it, then looked at Cynthia. "Sorry about that. Didn't want to lose my place."

"No problem. I've been there myself," Cynthia said, remembering how frustrating it was to lose her place in a long run of calculations. "I'm Cynthia Webber, from the Calgary Police Service." She extended her hand to Sherie, and Sherie accepted it.

From the many photos on her desk and the gentleness with which she'd engaged with Cynthia, she guessed Sherie was a mom. She hoped she'd been close to Maris.

"Well, I've already told Detective Bain everything I could think of about Maris. I sure do miss her. And not just her help here at work. It's not like her not to come to work. I can't help but think something terrible has happened to her." Yes, Cynthia couldn't help jumping to the same conclusion herself after having read Maris's journal, but she was happy to find a coworker who Maris may have trusted enough to confide in.

"Is this Maris's desk?" Cynthia asked pointing to the desk next to Sherie's.

"Yes. A lot of the bookkeeping tasks Maris and I do are connected, so it's handy having her right next to me."

"Are you the Horsemen's Bookkeeper then?"

"Yes, and Maris is my assistant."

"And what are your main duties?"

"We take care of the payments to the horse owners and trainers as well as the winnings payouts to our gamblers . . . uh . . . patrons." Sherie's cheeks turned a bit pink.

"What about the casino? Are you responsible for the casino books too?"

"Goodness, no. There's a casino bookkeeping team down the hall. Maris, Vivian, and I can barely keep up with the racetrack stuff. Well, technically, as the CFO, Vivian oversees the casino records too."

Cynthia nodded then looked around to see if they were alone.

The receptionist had gone back to her desk. There was a door leading to an office at the back of the bullpen. She pulled out the chair at Maris's desk, sat down, and leaned a little closer to Sherie. She lowered her voice.

"Is that Vivian's office?" She pointed to the office at the back.

"Yes. She's not in right now though." Sherie seemed to guess what Cynthia was thinking as she pointed to a desk against the wall beside the entrance to Vivian's office. "And that desk over there is a spare. Vivian's been saying for months she's going to hire another bookkeeper, but that hasn't happened yet." Sherie sighed and rolled her eyes. Cynthia nodded again, sympathizing with Sherie's frustrations with her boss.

"Are all the computers connected to the network?" Cynthia asked.

"As far as I know. You could check with Todd. He's our tech guru."

"Perfect. Okay, I'm going to look through Maris's desk and check some things on her computer. I was hoping to talk to Vivian, but this subpoena has everything she needs to know. I'll leave a copy on her desk before I go if she hasn't turned up by then." Cynthia took out a notepad and jotted down some things she wanted to remember, like the computer tech's name.

"Feel free to interrupt me if you need anything, dear," Sherie said, putting her head down and getting back to work. It was just a few seconds before Cynthia interrupted her.

"Actually, I know you said you've already talked to Detective Bain, but would you mind coming by the station later?" Cynthia sensed Sherie may open up more about her boss if she was out of the office.

"Of course. Anything to help Maris. I can stop by after work."

"That's great! Thank you, Sherie. Here's my card in case anything comes up before then."

"Thank you, dear." Sherie opened a desk drawer, pulled out one of her own cards, and gave it to Cynthia in exchange.

18

Back at his office, Randy Bain was shuffling through papers on his desk searching for the laptop buried beneath them while ignoring the rumblings of his stomach that told him coffee wasn't enough to get him to lunch.

"Hello, handsome." Randy looked up even though he recognized the sultry voice. He wished it was anyone else.

"How did you get back here?"

"Don't worry, nobody saw me," Vivian replied. "Didn't you have a good time last night, Detective?"

Randy's ears and cheeks burned. "Sure, but you're not supposed to be back here, and it's best if we keep whatever this is," he gestured at Vivian then back to himself, "between us."

"Oh, please. You know exactly what this is. We each have something the other wants." She took a step closer. Her blouse was buttoned one button too low, and the black lace of her bra was peeking out. "It's not my fault we don't want the same things. I think it's a fair trade though, don't you?"

He sighed as Vivian stepped closer. They were almost face to face. "Come on. It's a really bad idea, your being here. Anyone passing by at the right time could see you in here." He gestured at his office window. It looked out into a hallway where more windows spanned the full height of the wall. The hallway ran parallel to the outside walkway that led from the parking lot to the front entrance of the station.

"Yeah," she glanced over her shoulder and out into the parking lot. "It's really too bad you have so many windows in this place," she said, untucking Randy's shirt and running a finger from his hip to his belly button.

"I have an idea," he said tucking his shirt back into his pants, grabbing Vivian's hand, and leading her to the hall. Randy poked his head out into the hallway, checking for coworkers. "Come on," he said, and they disappeared down the hall towards the back entrance.

***

Twenty minutes later, Randy reappeared in the same hallway, alone. He glanced down to find his shirt wasn't buttoned properly and stepped into his office to make an adjustment before heading to the reception area at the front of the building.

"Excuse me, Wanda," he said. Wanda looked up from her typing.

"Are you all right, Detective? You look a little flushed."

"Yes, I . . . uh . . . just got back from a run." He suddenly felt the need to take a shower. "Anyway, did you see a woman come through here, maybe thirty minutes ago?" He flipped through the clipboard on the reception desk where visitors were required to sign in.

"No, Detective. Nobody in the last hour. Are you expecting someone?"

"Not exactly." He saw the confused expression on Wanda's face and figured it was as good a place as any to end the conversation. "Thanks, Wanda." He tapped the visitor log twice with his index and middle fingers and headed back to his office. He had underestimated Vivian, and he wished he'd done a more thorough background check before getting into bed with her.

19

It had been nearly two hours since Cynthia first set foot in the administration offices of Cooper Downs. Getting access to Maris's computer wasn't as easy as she'd hoped. Maris was very particular about her passwords and hadn't written them down in any obvious locations.

Cynthia had discovered Maris's Cooper Downs pass card in the top drawer of her desk while searching for a notebook or piece of paper that might have contained her passwords.

Todd, the tech guy, eventually came to reset the password on Maris's computer so Cynthia could look for confirmation of what Maris had noted in her journal about the duplicate winning tickets. Once Cynthia was able to log in to Maris's computer and access the Cooper Downs network, it took her some time to get acquainted with the software they used for their accounting. It was a proprietary program developed especially for the horse-racing industry, and Cynthia had never seen it before.

She had to interrupt Sherie a few more times to find out how to view sales journals and use the search function, and Sherie was more than happy to give her a quick rundown. After checking back in Maris's journal to make sure she had the correct ticket numbers, Cynthia was able to locate the tickets, but there was no evidence duplicate tickets had been printed. Cynthia's first thought was someone had gone back into the system and deleted the duplicates.

"I'm sorry to interrupt you again," she said to Sherie, "but is a ticket sales summary printed at the end of each day?"

"Don't worry about it. When Vivian's here, I get interrupted all the time."

"Is she normally gone for long periods like this?" Cynthia asked.

"Only when she has lunch meetings."

Cynthia nodded. Today must be one of those days.

"So, yes, we do print sales journals every day. We keep a paper copy in the binders in Vivian's office. They're organized by date." Sherie pushed her chair away from her desk and stood. "I can show you where they are."

Cynthia stood and followed Sherie into Vivian's office. "All these blue binders are full of daily sales reports organized by date," said Sherie, pointing to the bottom two shelves of a bookcase in Vivian's office. "But you might find it easier to search the back-up copies stored as PDFs on our network."

"Yes, that sounds like it might save me some time."

"Also in the blue binders, you'll find the winning tickets that have been claimed and paid," Sherie said over her shoulder as she walked back to her desk with Cynthia in tow.

What a lifesaver Sherie was. Using the search function in the PDF files made the hunt for the duplicate tickets go a lot faster. The PDFs were saved by date, which Cynthia knew based on the sales journal reports in the accounting program. She found the three ticket numbers she was looking for, each in separate PDF documents. Again, there was no evidence of duplicate tickets and the sequencing of the ticket numbers appeared correct. She copied the documents to the flash drive she'd brought with her.

While she had the subpoena with her, which granted her access to everything she needed to look at, Cynthia really wanted to talk with Vivian before accessing the physical records in her office. She needed to view the printouts of the same documents she'd just viewed on the network, and she'd need the physical tickets too. It would be nice to establish some professional courtesy and get a read on whether or not Vivian put any stock in the concerns Maris had voiced. Cynthia would have to come back and look at the printed copies of the documents when she could talk to Vivian about accessing her office.

Cynthia stared at Maris's computer monitor, the wheels in

her head churning. She'd done all she could without searching the records in Vivian's office. Leaving only to come back later seemed silly, but waiting around for Vivian was a waste of time, and time was of the essence. She logged off Maris's computer and told Sherie she'd be back soon.

***

Back at the station, Cynthia couldn't decide if she'd made the right decision. Should she have ventured into Vivian's office and taken what she needed rather than waiting? She couldn't stop thinking about the keycard in Maris's desk drawer. She wandered down the hall to Detective Bain's office, hoping to get his opinion.

"Hey, Randy," she said from the doorway. "Do you have a minute?"

"Of course, what's up?" Randy said, looking up from his desk.

"Does it seem strange to you that Maris would leave her Cooper Downs keycard in her desk?"

Randy paused as if thinking about his answer. "Not really. It was probably a spare."

"Hmmm, okay. Sorry to bother you."

Cynthia wasn't convinced.

"Funny we didn't see it before though," Randy added, returning his focus to his laptop. "Did you bring it back with you? We should probably analyze it for evidence."

Dammit, she should have just grabbed it. Her face went hot at the thought of screwing up.

"No, but I need to get back out there. The CFO, uh . . . Vivian," she paused, waiting for a reaction from Randy that never came. His eyes remained glued to his laptop. "She wasn't around, and I'd really like to get her take on Maris's suspicions."

"Make sure you grab that keycard." This time Randy looked up. His eyes met hers with a cold stare. "I know missing persons isn't your area. If you're not sure if something is important, err on the side of caution."

Cynthia's glance fell to the grey industrial carpet covering the floor in Randy's office. She mumbled in agreement then fled Randy's office, annoyed she'd messed up her first trip to Cooper Downs.

20

Back at her desk, Cynthia began making notes about her morning at Cooper Downs and planning her next steps. She thought of Linda again and wondered if she'd woken up yet. Linda probably would have grabbed that keycard. Cynthia sighed as she pulled out her phone and dialed Linda's mom.

There was no change. Cynthia's energy shifted and a sense of duty overwhelmed her. The trepidations of investigating Maris's disappearance melted away. Not only would she help find Maris, but she'd figure out who hurt Linda too. She couldn't afford to make any more sloppy mistakes. She needed to keep moving forward. It was time to visit Harvey.

The second floor of police headquarters was abuzz with activity. It was one of the largest and most respected municipal police services in Canada. Every day since she'd started three months ago, Cynthia saw faces she didn't recognize. Rows of desks with computers and room dividers were laid out like a human maze. She found Harvey's desk and stood silently beside it, examining him while he pounded away on his keyboard.

"Hey, doll," he said when he looked up from his computer screen.

Cynthia flashed a smile and blushed. She couldn't help it, even though she knew he called all the women at headquarters "doll". They all put up with it because he was harmless. The few times Cynthia had seen him in the lunchroom, she'd thought he was actually quite shy when he wasn't at his desk. Today he had on a pair of computer glasses with yellow lenses and thick black frames. They made him look like a giant bug.

"Could you take a look at this?" she said, holding up the flash drive containing the PDF documents she'd copied from Cooper

Downs's network. "Please," she added. She'd been working on manners with Luke, and it made her acutely aware of her own tone.

"Of course. What you got?"

Cynthia gave Harvey the rundown of the suspected ticket fraud and told him she was looking for any sort of electronic document editing or tampering in the files. Since there was no evidence of duplicate ticket numbers on the PDF, she wondered if someone could have removed them.

"Is there any way you can check the Cooper Downs network?"

"Well, they don't call me Hack for nothing. You got the necessary paperwork?"

"Of course. I'll forward it to you when I get back to my desk."

"You want me to see if there's evidence of someone deleting information from the server?"

"Yes, exactly. The PDFs on that jump drive may have been tampered with as well. I'll send you the reports and dates with a copy of the subpoena."

"All right, doll. I'm ready to rock and roll as soon as you say the word."

"Thanks, Harvey." Cynthia started to leave, but Harvey called her back.

"You know, you're the only one around here that calls me that."

"It's how Louise introduced you. Harvey Ackerman."

"Sure, but even she calls me Hack."

"Hackerman," an officer said and nodded to Harvey as he walked by.

"Joe," Harvey said as he nodded back.

"Wow," Cynthia said, her face suddenly brightening. "I just realized your name is your job. I thought everyone called you Hack because you're so good, but that's *actually* your name. How did I not see that before?" Cynthia's eyes widened, and she mouthed the word "wow" again as she shook her head slowly from side to side.

Harvey chuckled a little. "Yes, it's my name, and I *am* that good." This time he was completely serious. "There's only one person I know as good as me in this city—Kelinda White. She was a year ahead of me in the computer science program. I . . . uh . . . kind of had a crush on her. She was legendary." Harvey looked down at his desk and cleared his throat.

"Uh, back to the point I was making." He looked up at Cynthia from his chair. "You and I have been working together for a while now. There's no need to be so formal."

"I'm sorry, I—"

"It's forgotten already," Harvey cut her off. He held up the flash drive. "I'll get back to you on this asap." And with that, Cynthia ran back down to the main floor to get ready for her return trip to Cooper Downs.

21

As soon as she sat down at her desk and opened her laptop to email Hack the information he needed, Wanda buzzed her desk phone.

"Cynthia? Sherie Richards is here from Cooper Downs."

"Thanks, Wanda. I'll be right there."

Reflecting on her conversation with Randy earlier, it was clear to Cynthia there was only one thing she needed to know from Sherie. She strolled to reception then escorted Sherie back to her office.

She'd already gotten most of the information she needed when she was at Cooper Downs, but she was hoping Sherie would be more forthcoming with information about Vivian, especially now that she was at the police station, behind closed doors, without the risk of Vivian walking in at any moment.

Sherie paused to put her greying hair up in a clip before taking a seat in one of the chairs in front of Cynthia's desk. Then she used her hand to fan her face.

"Can I get you some water?" Cynthia asked.

"I'm all right, dear. Just a hot flash. It'll pass soon enough."

Cynthia wasn't sure what to say, so she thanked Sherie for coming in and asked her if she'd thought of anything else since they'd last spoken.

"Well," Sherie paused and looked over her shoulder at the closed door.

"It's okay, Sherie. Anything you tell me is held in the strictest confidence, and it could help us figure out what happened to Maris."

"Maris told me about the duplicate ticket numbers she found.

She asked me what she should do about them." Sherie fidgeted with her hands as she spoke then fanned her face again. "I told her it was probably just a transposition error, but she wanted to make sure Vivian knew anyway. She told me afterwards Vivian didn't seem to care."

"Did this surprise you?"

Sherie stared at Cynthia's desk as if she was thinking carefully about her answer.

"Vivian is . . . ah . . ." Sherie took a breath in through her nose, "interesting," she said as she exhaled. "She's very busy overseeing the accounting department and putting out all the fires her son starts. I'm not surprised it seemed like she didn't care."

"Her son? Is that Paul?"

"Yes. He works in security. Thinks he can rough up anyone who looks at him funny. Vivian's always making excuses for him and coming to his rescue with HR. I'm sure he would have been fired by now if it wasn't for her."

"Maris mentioned Paul in her journal. She wrote about two other men but didn't say much about them. It seemed like they might have been friends with Paul. Do you know who they might be?"

Sherie shook her head. "Sorry."

"Were you ever asked to attend after-hours parties for high rollers and horse owners?" Cynthia wasn't sure if the blank expression on Sherie's face was shock or bewilderment, so she explained further.

"Apparently Vivian threatened to fire Maris if she didn't dress sexy and attend these parties."

"I wouldn't know anything about that. I'm sure I'm not their type. I'm married and, well . . ." She gestured at her ageing, lumpy body.

"Does it seem odd to you Vivian would threaten Maris like that?"

"Not really. Like I mentioned, Vivian is interesting. She threatens us on a daily basis. None of us take it seriously. We just think she's being a bitch." Sherie's hand flew to her mouth. "I'm sorry, I shouldn't have said that."

Cynthia smiled. "That's perfectly all right. You've been very helpful. I just have one more question for you." Sherie's posture relaxed a little, and the redness in her face eased. "How many keycards does Cooper Downs issue to their employees?"

"Just one." Sherie looked confused. "Why would we need extra keycards?"

"And you need your keycard to access the employee-only areas at Cooper Downs, don't you?"

"Yes, absolutely."

"Can you think of any reason Maris's keycard would be in her desk?" Finally, the only question Cynthia really wanted to ask Sherie.

"No, Maris always wore her card on a lanyard around her neck. She would never leave it in her desk." Sherie's expression switched from confusion to concern.

Cynthia finished typing and skimmed her notes while Sherie sat in silence. "Thank you so much, Sherie. That's all I have for you." Cynthia stood and Sherie did the same. They walked to the reception area where Cynthia reminded Sherie she could call any time if she remembered anything else.

As she rushed back to her desk, Cynthia obsessed about Maris's keycard, hoping it would still be there by the time she got back to Cooper Downs. It was 4:30 p.m. now. With it being rush hour, she wasn't sure if she would make it back to Cooper Downs before the administration office closed, but she had to try. If Maris hadn't put the card in her desk, hopefully whoever did had left their prints behind.

22

When Cynthia arrived at Cooper Downs, the dinner rush was just starting. She knew the administration offices would be closing soon and had to hurry if she was going to get a good look at Maris's drawer.

The main administration office door was open, and although she found it odd, she was relieved no one was around. She went straight to Maris's desk and opened the drawer where she had seen the keycard. It was still attached to Maris's lanyard, which she pulled out of the drawer. She was careful not to touch the card with her fingers.

As she was about to close the drawer, she saw the face of her best friend staring back at her. Her mouth gaped and her eyebrows raised. Why was Linda's S-CAL keycard in Maris's desk? She felt a queasiness in her stomach. Maybe Linda had dropped it when they were having dinner the other night? But how would it end up here? She grabbed the card, also by its lanyard, and hoped her friend would wake up from her coma soon so Cynthia could get to the bottom of this. She carefully tucked both cards into her laptop bag.

Because the administration office was deserted, Cynthia thought it was the perfect time to check Vivian's office for the physical copies of the reports and tickets she was looking for. She would have preferred to talk to Vivian first, but because she didn't want to risk missing further evidence, this would have to do. She knocked on the door to be sure nobody was inside before she opened it.

Vivian's office was bright and sunny thanks to a window behind and to the left of her desk. Framed photographs of horses and jockeys covered the walls. Cynthia focused on the photos. It was hard to tell, but it appeared to be the same jockey in all of them. She laid a copy of the subpoena on Vivian's desk and went to the binders Sherie had shown her earlier. She took a quick look over her shoulder then began taking binders off the shelf, first looking for the ticket stubs.

Winning tickets that had been claimed and paid out were taped to sheets of loose-leaf paper and stored numerically in the binders. Accompanying the paid tickets was the paperwork indicating who had claimed the funds, along with their address and signature. Now to find the tickets she was looking for. A faint noise came from outside the office. Cynthia glanced out the window, listening. Vivian's office door clicked shut.

"Hello?" Cynthia called out. "Is someone there?" Must be the janitor. She walked to the door to find out who it was. When she grasped the doorknob, it turned, but the door wouldn't budge. Odd, since she'd noticed the door didn't have a lock. She pounded on the door with her open palm. It bowed slightly as if something had been wedged in place to keep her from getting out. A purple trench coat hung on the back of the door. Had Vivian locked her in? Why? Was she still in the building somewhere? She tried the door again. It still wouldn't budge.

"Seriously," Cynthia said to no one. She opted not to panic just yet. She was on a mission after all. If she could find out who was scamming the racetrack, she'd be closer to finding Maris, and maybe even Linda's assaulter. She'd get the evidence she came for, then worry about getting out of there.

Cynthia turned her attention back to the binders by the window. She made a mental note that the window opened, but being on the second floor with nothing but pavement to break her fall would cause serious bodily harm if she had to exit that way.

To Cynthia's frustration, the binders on Vivian's bookshelf weren't labeled with the date ranges of the tickets they contained. After three tries, she found the binders containing all the winning tickets for the last six months. But the tickets Maris mentioned in her journal were at least eight months old.

She tried a couple more binders and found August 2017, the month Maris found the first ticket. She pulled out her phone to find the exact numbers of the three tickets she was looking for. Her thumb swiped across her phone, causing her call history to pop up. She saw Ben's number, hesitated, then pressed "Call" anyway. She felt butterflies in her stomach. She hated that they'd fought the last time they'd seen each other.

Her heart raced while the phone rang. Did Ben really not want her to call? Surely he'd be willing to help her, wouldn't he? Ben would likely be walking home from D&A, the best international accounting firm in Calgary, he always said. His voicemail kicked in, and she took a deep breath before hearing the familiar beep to leave a message.

"Hey. I know you're pissed at me, but I could really use your help right now. I'm stuck in the CFO's office at Cooper Downs. I think someone is trying to keep me here. Never a dull moment. Call me when you get this." Cynthia hung up then scrolled to where she had made a note of the ticket numbers she was looking for. She checked the numbers against the binder. There was a blank space where the first ticket should have been.

Somebody had gotten there before her.

After the ordeal with PPC months ago, she was prepared for almost anything, but knowing someone had been there before her combined with the fact she was now trapped in Vivian's office tied her stomach in knots.

Who else could she call for help? She tried Randy's cell but didn't bother leaving a message when his voicemail kicked in. The last thing she wanted was him thinking she'd screwed up again. She found where the other two tickets should have been. The second one was also missing, but the third was intact. To her untrained eye, the ticket looked exactly like the tickets next to it. If it was a fake, it was a damn good one. Cynthia took the entire page out of the binder along with the paperwork signed by the winner. She stuck the papers in a folder she had in her laptop bag, hoping to preserve them as they were.

As she debated either jumping out the window or calling her parents to come to her rescue, she heard a scraping sound at the door. It sounded like someone dragging something heavy across the industrial carpet. Oh God, don't let me be locked in here all night. Cynthia felt her stomach turn again, and she inhaled deeply, trying to calm herself. There was a thump on the door, and it flung open.

23

Cynthia found herself staring up at the burly woman she'd seen arguing with Paul earlier. Up close, she looked to be in her mid-twenties, and she was at least a foot taller than Cynthia.

"I'm so sorry. Are you all right?" she said.

"Yeah, I'm fine," Cynthia lied. She wasn't sure she could trust this woman.

"I'm Kelly White. I work in the stables." She held her right hand out to Cynthia, and Cynthia couldn't help admire Kelly's biceps, thinking if she was built like that, she'd have been able to push her way out of Vivian's office herself. She accepted Kelly's hand and gave it a shake.

"I was late with my timesheet and thought I'd leave it on Vivian's desk, but someone wedged a chair under the handle and put the spare desk in front of it for good measure." Kelly pointed to a chair Cynthia hadn't noticed when she'd arrived. It looked like it belonged in the restaurant.

"Thank you. Your timing couldn't have been better. It appears someone didn't want me to leave." Cynthia dug in her bag for a business card and held it out for Kelly. "Cynthia Webber. I work with the police."

Kelly took the card and looked at it for a few seconds.

"Financial crimes, huh?"

"That's right." Cynthia paused before asking, "Did you know Maris Kane?"

Kelly looked at the floor before answering, "Not really. I know who she is. That's about it. Seen her picture on the news a lot lately." Kelly's eyes met Cynthia's again. "Is that why you're here?"

"Partly. If you think of any details that might help us find her, you have my number. I'm sorry, but I need to get home to my son." Cynthia turned sideways and stepped around Kelly to get through the doorway of Vivian's office as Kelly backed up to make room for her to pass.

Cynthia glanced over her shoulder at Kelly. "Thanks again for letting me out. I was a minute away from jumping out that window."

"That could have ended badly," Kelly replied. "How's your friend doing?"

Cynthia froze. "My friend?" she asked as she turned to face Kelly, waiting for her response.

"That reporter. I thought I saw you two having dinner last night."

Cynthia stepped closer to Kelly and glanced around the office before lowering her voice. "Did you leave that note?" She wasn't sure if she should be scared or grateful.

Kelly's cheeks flushed. "I, uh . . . saw on the news she was hurt pretty bad." Cynthia's phone beeped. She didn't have time for this run around.

"I'm sorry, I really need go." She reached into her bag and checked her phone as she headed out of the administration office. It was a text from Mom.

Everything okay? It read.

Shoot. She hadn't called to let her know she was going to be late picking up Luke. She quickly texted back.

On my way.

***

Cynthia hurried down the steps to the main floor of the casino and almost smacked straight into Paul for the second time that day. She looked up and caught his glare.

"Sorry," she said, not waiting for a response. All she wanted to do was get to her car then get Luke, but she'd need to drop off the keycards and documents she had stashed in her bag at the forensic lab on her way. Best to get them processing as soon as possible.

The parking lot had filled in the hour she'd been upstairs. She tried to remember where she'd parked as she felt a wave of light-headedness come over her. Then she spotted it—her red Focus. She sprinted to her car, popped inside, and locked the doors. When she looked up, she saw Paul at the edge of the parking lot, walking in the same direction she'd come from. She slunk down in her seat, holding her breath and waiting for him to leave.

24

It seemed to be taking forever for Cynthia's day to end. Cooper Downs was northeast of the city. Most of the thirty-minute drive to the Forensic Crime Scene Unit building was highway driving, but it was clearly rush hour. Thankfully, the FCSU building wasn't far from where her parents lived in the southeast, just outside the downtown core. Soon she'd be able to see Luke and give him a great big hug.

A squad car blaring its siren and flashing its lights passed in the oncoming lane. Cynthia glanced in her rearview mirror then back to the road in front of her. Hearing the siren getting closer instead of farther away, she glanced in the rearview again. The squad car pulled a U-turn several cars behind her. She slowed down and signalled to her right to let the car pass, but it pulled someone over before reaching her. She carried on her way, focusing on the traffic and forgetting about the squad car.

∗∗∗

Detective Bain was just leaving the office when he got a complaint of an erratic driver not far from the casino. Thinking it had been a while since he'd stopped a speeder, he jumped at the chance to take it. He merged onto the highway and headed south in the direction of the casino. It wasn't long before he spotted the erratic driver and had to pull a U-turn to position himself to pull the car over. He thanked God several cars actually stopped to let him in and the highway divider was only grass at that point along the highway. Now, if people would just pull over already. Could they not hear the siren?

The maniac behind the wheel had been easy to spot, but he clearly didn't want to stop for Randy. It really bugged him how sports car owners thought they could drive as fast as they wanted just because they had a car that could handle it. Where was this guy going in such a hurry? He managed to get even with the newer model black Camaro. He signalled with his hands a few times and was about to use the loud speaker when the guy finally slowed down and pulled to the side of the road.

Relieved that no accidents lay in the wake of this maniac, Randy got out of the squad car, keeping his eye on the driver through the sideview mirror as he approached. He was always alert and ready to grab his service weapon if necessary. Thankfully, the driver seemed pretty cooperative. He was ready with his licence and registration.

"Sorry, officer. I didn't see you there," the driver said, lowering his shades so he could make eye contact with Detective Bain who took his documents.

"I guess you were pretty focused on wherever you were going in such a hurry. Do you know how fast you were going?"

The driver laughed. "No idea, man."

Randy read the driver's licence—Paul Lennings—then the registration–Vivian Lennings. Shit. He was going to have to let this bastard off.

"Borrowed your mom's car, did you?" Randy handed the documents back to Paul, who was wearing a security uniform.

"What's it to you?" Paul snorted and snatched the documents from Randy.

"You might want to treat a beautiful car like this with some respect, and maybe pay a little closer attention to the speed signs. How would your mom feel if you totalled her car?"

"Aw, she'd just buy another one." Randy's mouth gaped, and he raised his eyebrows.

"Well, I'd tell you to slow down, but I think you're going to do what you want anyway. Consider this your warning."

Paul had already put the Camaro in gear.

"Warning, huh?" Paul leaned out the window and lowered his shades to make eye contact with Randy again. "You can't touch me, and you know it." His tone had lost its cooperative feel.

"Screw you, cop!" Paul said, squealing the tires and nearly running over Randy's foot as he pulled away from the curb.

25

After her ordeal at the casino and dropping the evidence off with the forensic team, Cynthia was almost an hour late getting to her parents' house to pick up Luke. Mom rushed to the door, holding it open for Cynthia when she arrived.

"Everything, okay?" she asked, echoing her text from earlier and hugging Cynthia.

"Sorry, Mom." Cynthia refrained from explaining what had happened when she caught Luke running into the room out of the corner of her eye. She glanced at Luke then back to Mom.

"You're here now. I just worry about you after the whole . . ." Gayle lowered her voice and looked at Luke, " . . . David fiasco."

"I know, Mom." Cynthia's former boss had turned out to be a maniacal psychopath. The memory of his beady little eyes and nicotine-stained teeth still made her stomach lurch. She gave her head a quick shake to release the memory.

"I'm fine, really. There's a whole force of officers I can call on at any time." But she'd only called Randy. Thankfully Kelly had rescued her before she'd needed to call anyone else. Mom didn't need to know that.

"Then Ben called, and I really started to worry," Mom added. Cynthia's eyes widened at the mention of Ben.

"He did?"

"Yeah, probably not even fifteen minutes ago. Said he was going to the hospital to check on Linda and wondered if he might see you there."

He must have seen the news. "I need to see her." Cynthia knelt down so she could look her son in the eyes. "You want to go check on Auntie Linda with me?"

"Yeah." Luke's eyes sparkled and his lips curled into a smile.

"She might be sleeping still, but we'll go find out." Cynthia and Mom exchanged concerned looks. "Okay, go find your coat. I'm going to grab a snack." In an effort to quiet her grumbling stomach, Cynthia searched her parents' snack cupboard above the cutlery drawer. "You mind if I take this?" She looked over her shoulder at Mom while holding up a granola bar.

"Of course, anything you like. Leftovers are in the fridge if you want something more substantial."

"It's all right. This is portable."

"You can leave Luke here, you know. Are you sure you want to drag him to the hospital?"

"He'll be fine. Plus, if Linda's awake, I know he'll cheer her up."

"Suit yourself." Mom shrugged and busied herself with the dishes in the sink.

***

Cynthia wasn't sure what she was going to find when she got to the hospital. She'd hoped Linda's parents would call her if there was any news, but they had enough on their minds. Cynthia was glad she had Luke for company. He didn't seem as negatively affected by the hospital as she was, not as impacted by all the pain, all the lives coming and going.

She hoped Linda wasn't in any pain. She'd looked peaceful enough hooked up to the monitors. It was a good sign Linda could breathe on her own. Her gut told her Linda would be back to her old self soon. As they got closer to Linda's room, Cynthia heard voices. She sped up a little, Luke in tow, and strained to hear if her friend's voice was one of them. Her heart beat faster, and her mouth suddenly went dry with anticipation. As she turned into Room 252, Cynthia saw Linda sitting up in bed, most of the machines removed except an IV line and a vital-signs monitor.

"You're back!" Cynthia hurried to the edge of Linda's bed and hugged her delicately then looked to Linda's parents, who filled her in on Linda's progress.

Linda's skin was ashen, and her lips looked dry and pale. She looked as if she'd been up for days even though Linda's parents said she'd only been fully awake for the last twenty minutes. A nurse arrived just as Linda opened her mouth to say something.

"I'm sorry, people. Looks like the party's just getting started, but Ms. Reeves here needs her rest. Anybody who isn't family needs to come back tomorrow." The nurse, who seemed to have no regard for personal space, pushed her way to the vitals monitor. Luke tucked himself behind Cynthia.

"It's okay, buddy." Cynthia reassured him with a pat on the shoulder then grabbed Linda's hand. "We'll be back. Promise me you'll listen to the nurses and get some rest?"

Linda nodded then cleared her throat. "Ben was looking for you." She spoke slower and softer than usual.

"Oh, yeah." Linda's mother chimed in. "He seemed worried, dear. You just missed him."

"Thanks. I'll give him a call," Cynthia said as she gave each of Linda's parents a hug and turned to leave.

"Bye, Auntie Linda," Luke said waving. Linda smiled and waved back.

***

Cynthia buckled Luke into his car seat. She knew it wouldn't be long before he was snoozing on the forty-minute drive, and sure enough, by the time they arrived home, Luke was passed out in the backseat. Cynthia took a minute to check her messages. She hadn't remembered checking her voicemail since before she was stuck in Vivian's office. The first message was Ben.

"Can we just forget about what happened last night? I care about you Cynthia, and when I get messages like the one I got from you today . . . I just don't want to lose you." Cynthia dialed Ben's number, thinking about the message she'd left him from

Vivian's office. Her call went straight to voicemail again, and she waited for his outgoing message to end before speaking.

"Yes, let's forget about last night. I'm sorry I was hard on you the other night. It's not like you go out with Ryan that often, and . . . I miss you." She pressed the red button on her phone to end the call and put it in her coat pocket.

After she'd put Luke to bed, Cynthia thought more about being trapped in Vivian's office. It hadn't seemed like a big deal at the time, but with a bit of distance, she was having a hard time making sense of it all. All kinds of questions ran through her mind—who would do that? And why keep her there? What could they possibly accomplish?

She concluded whoever had done it must have planned to come back. The thought sent a shiver up her spine. It was time to talk to Randy about getting a service weapon.

26

Since sleep was a fleeting notion, Cynthia had taken Luke over to Mom and Dad's as soon as he was up. Her parents were early risers, and they had become Luke's primary caregivers during the day since she'd started working for the police. By the time Randy arrived at the station, Cynthia had already received a forensics report on the keycards. They proved to be a dead end. Either whoever had touched the keycards wasn't in the system, or they had taken great care not to get their prints on them.

As Cynthia reviewed her notes from yesterday, she realized the list of things she had to talk to Randy about was growing quickly: the keycards, Vivian's office, the missing tickets. Best to catch him now before he got busy for the day. She hustled down the hall, notes in hand, and tapped on Randy's door.

"Yeah," Randy said, without looking up.

"You got a minute for a quick update on the Maris Kane case?" Cynthia stepped into Randy's office, noticing a pungent smell as if Randy had spent the night at the station, though she'd just seen him come in.

"Come in, come in." Randy motioned for Cynthia to sit down but still didn't make eye contact. He was rifling through the papers on top of his desk as if looking for something, as usual.

"Someone locked me in Vivian Lenning's office when I was at Cooper Downs looking for evidence yesterday."

"What?" Randy stopped shuffling papers and sat down behind his desk. "Is that why you called me yesterday? Why didn't you leave a message?"

"I'm sure you have better things to do than drop everything and open a door for me. Besides, I wasn't trapped in there long.

Luckily, one of the stable hands forgot to submit her hours for payroll, and she let me out."

Randy slid his hands over his face then through his greasier than usual hair. "Okay. What else?"

"I dropped some evidence off at the FCSU building. Linda's keycard was in Maris's desk drawer. Along with Maris's. I think whoever put it there put Linda in the hospital."

"Jesus. Seems like a logical conclusion. See, you've got a keen sense of observation. So what if it's normally directed at numbers? You're doing fine with this case." Cynthia wasn't sure if Randy meant to make her feel better, or if he was trying to convince himself it was okay to have a forensic accountant doing an investigator's job.

"That's not all. I found one of the duplicate winning tickets. The other two were missing. I don't know who has access to Vivian's office, and she's impossible to get a hold of, but it looks like we might be dealing with an inside job."

"Hmm." Randy's gaze drifted out into the hallway as if he was thinking about what he wanted to say next. "Where is the ticket now?"

"The lab. I took more than just that one ticket. Thought it would be good to compare to the other tickets in the series and see if there are any clues as to how or where the duplicate ticket was printed."

"Seems odd the duplicate ticket would end up in the ticket book with the rest of the winning tickets, doesn't it?"

"No. All the winning tickets need to be accounted for to balance the payouts to winners. Maris was probably the one who put the tickets in the book, which is why she noticed the duplicates. It's possible Vivian's the one who removed those tickets."

Randy nodded. "She is the obvious suspect since she has access to all the accounting records."

Cynthia couldn't remember what else she wanted to tell Randy. She checked her notes. Looked like she got it all. Thank God. The smell of Randy's body odour was starting to give her a headache. Were those the same clothes he wore yesterday?

"You look like you could use a coffee," she said, wringing her fingers, hoping he hadn't noticed she was inspecting him.

"Thanks, but I've got to head out. As soon as I find my notepad." He stood up and started shuffling papers again.

"I'll leave you to it."

"Nice work," said Randy as Cynthia left his office. She couldn't help but think the compliment was an afterthought.

***

"What the hell?" Randy hissed into his cellphone while he sat in a cruiser in the station parking lot. "If you want me to keep my end of the deal, you've got to promise me my employees will be safe."

Randy wished there was another way out of his financial mess. He had no business putting the responsibility of a missing person's case, especially one with a dead end, on Cynthia. Goddamn Vivian. At least the cases were related. He just hoped Cynthia was scared enough to stay away from Cooper Downs for a while. At least until he could see his plan through. It was time to check in with Kat and see how she was doing with the supplies he needed.

27

Cynthia heard tires squeal outside the station as she headed towards the break room. When she entered the breakroom, Officer Warren Scott was pouring himself a coffee.

"Morning, Warren," Cynthia said cheerily as she plugged in the electric tea kettle and grabbed a tea bag and cup out of the cupboard. "Have you talked to Randy this morning?"

"No, why?"

"He seems a little on edge. Maybe like he didn't sleep last night."

"Probably just the usual stress of the job. There's more open cases than usual right now." Warren poured some milk in his coffee and took a sip. His face relaxed and his shoulders dropped an inch. "Speaking of which, I better get back to it," he said, putting the lid on his travel mug and nodding at Cynthia. He turned his large frame sideways to let Hack pass through the break room entrance.

"See you later," Cynthia said to the back of Warren's head while greeting Hack with a smile.

"Hey, doll," Hack said. "You were right about those PDFs you asked me to look at. Someone had altered them."

"Really?" Cynthia's eyes shone with anticipation. "Can you tell who altered them?"

"The document properties show Amarillis Kane was the last person to update the file," replied Hack.

"That doesn't make any sense. Why would she bring something like that to her boss if she was the one who changed it?"

"It would be easy enough for anyone with her network password to use her computer to make the change."

"Hmmm." Cynthia let out a sigh and looked down at the floor.

"Don't look so sad, doll. I wouldn't have come all the way down here with bad news."

Cynthia looked at Hack, who was only slightly taller than her. He was still wearing his funny yellow-lensed glasses even though they were only meant for viewing computer screens.

"Really?" she asked.

"Someone on the outside could also make that change and have it look like Maris did it. I checked the Cooper Downs network, and it was accessed from the outside at times corresponding to the dates on the winning tickets."

"That makes sense. Whoever did this would have to know the winning tickets weren't claimed, otherwise their plan wouldn't work," said Cynthia. She touched her finger to her lips for a moment and added, "I sent some tickets to the lab to see if they were printed on one of the Cooper Downs printers or somewhere else."

"Good thinking. Whoever hacked into the system used different IP addresses each time, but they all originate here in the city."

"Well, that makes sense since I would expect it to be someone local so they could easily pick up their prize money."

"True, but a hacker anywhere in the world can make it look like they're local if they know what they're doing," said Hack.

"So, we're really no further ahead than before?" asked Cynthia.

"I'm still analyzing the code used to get into the Cooper Downs network."

"The code?" Cynthia asked.

"Hackers often leave a signature, so they can brag about it to their cyber buddies. I'm sure I'll find some identifiers in the code."

Cynthia wasn't sure what Hack was talking about, but she trusted he would find a good lead for her. The kettle whistled, and Cynthia poured some boiling water on top of the tea bag in her mug. Hack helped himself to some foul-smelling coffee.

"I don't know how anyone can drink that stuff," said Cynthia, trying not to inhale the rancid coffee fumes.

Hack eyed Cynthia with a quizzical look then looked in her teacup.

"Likewise," he said, mixing copious amounts of cream and sugar into his coffee with a plastic stir stick.

Cynthia chuckled and picked up her mug. "Thanks for the update. Keep me posted on that code signature . . . thingy."

28

The day had gone by faster than usual, and Cynthia was no further ahead than she had been this morning. As she sat down at her desk, Cynthia reflected on what Louise had told her. Most occupational frauds were committed by employees in the accounting department or upper management. If she couldn't get Vivian to talk to her, she'd go above her head. She looked on the Cooper Downs website to find out who Vivian reported to. Looked like it was the big guys in Dallas. Dammit! She'd go nowhere fast trying to get Dallas involved.

She pulled out her cellphone to call Vivian again. The woman was impossible to pin down. Cynthia's phone indicated there was a message waiting for her. She dialed her voicemail and listened while tapping on her laptop, entering the password to access her police email account. The voicemail was from Ben, trying to arrange a date night. As his message ended, her phone beeped in her ear, alerting her to an incoming call. She connected the call without looking at the number.

"Cyn! You gotta get me out of here!" It was Linda, sounding much better than she'd looked last night.

"What the hell? Are you supposed to be making calls?" Cynthia was happy to hear from her friend but concerned she was going to push to get out of the hospital before she was ready.

"Oh, please. I'm fine. Just a little blurred vision and one mother of a headache." Cynthia rolled her eyes even though Linda couldn't see.

"Oh, yeah. Just a little blurry vision," Cynthia mocked. "You really should take it easy. You've suffered a brain injury. How did you get a phone in your room anyway?" Cynthia glanced at her laptop and the unopened mail in her email account that had loaded.

"Nurse Ratched is off today. Today's nurse . . . uh, I forget her name. Apparently, I may have some trouble with my memory for a while too. Anyway, she's a sweetheart. A big fan apparently—"

"Holy shit!" Cynthia cut in.

"What? You're surprised I have fans?"

"It's not that. Call me back in ten?" For the first time in her life, Cynthia hung up on her best friend and dialed Mom, her heart pounding in her ears. Thankfully, Mom answered on the first ring.

"Cynthia, I—"

"Mom," Cynthia tried not to sound as panicked as she felt. She wiped a sweaty hand on her pants. "I need you to do something, but I can't tell you why right now. Do you think you can handle that?"

"Uh," Mom hesitated but didn't answer.

"I need you and Dad to take Luke to the cabin and stay there until I can get out there. Can you do that?"

"Well, I'll have to cancel my card game, but yeah, we can do that."

"You can't tell anyone where you're going."

"Cynthia, are you okay? You're scaring me again."

"It's fine, Mom." Cynthia stared at the email that had triggered the call. "I just don't want to take any chances after what happened with David. I know you'll be safe at the cabin." The cabin was about an hour west of Calgary in Kananaskis country. Cynthia's fond memories of the cabin made it feel like her safe place.

"Okay, dear. I'll take my cell. Make sure you keep me posted, all right?" Her voice dropped off.

"I will. Try not to worry. It's just a precaution." Cynthia wasn't sure whether she was trying to convince herself or Mom.

"Don't you know mothers never stop worrying about their children?"

Oh, she knew. "So, you understand why I've asked you to go

then?" Cynthia asked.

"Of course. Any idea how long we'll need to stay out there?" Mom sounded like she'd resolved to trust her.

"I wish I did. I love you, Mom. Could you put Luke on, please?"

"Of course."

Cynthia took a deep breath and pictured Luke's face. Ever since Jason had died, he had an uncanny ability to tell when something was wrong. She smiled to herself, hoping it would hide the fear in her voice. She told Luke Grandma and Grandpa were taking him on a mini-vacation and she'd be joining them as soon as she could.

His voice told her he was excited, and she could picture him jumping up and down with his eyes wide open—the innocence of a four-year-old. Mission accomplished. She hoped Luke's excitement would keep Mom in good spirits too.

Another call came in as Cynthia was saying goodbye to Luke. "I love you, baby. I have to go now. See you soon."

She answered the call, instinctively knowing it was Linda calling her back.

"What's going on?" Linda's tone was serious this time.

"I'm sorry. I just got a . . . *death threat*."

"What? Are you fucking kidding me?"

"Do you think I would kid about that? I'll forward it." Cynthia paused, thinking about what she had just said. "Shit, I can't. It's evidence. I've got to get this to Randy . . . and Hack."

"I know this isn't the time for questions, but do you seriously have a guy named 'Hack' over there?"

The adrenaline rushing through her body caused Cynthia to laugh nervously. The sweat at her armpits was seeping through her blouse, and her face felt prickly and hot.

"That's what we call our cybercrimes guy. His name is Harvey Ackerman, but since he's a genius and hacks into computers for a living, he gets all kinds of nicknames. 'Hack' and 'Hackerman' are the nicer two."

"That's awesome." Linda giggled, and it calmed Cynthia a

little. "So, what's up with this death threat? Anything like the one I got last year?" Linda asked.

Trading stories about death threats was the last thing Cynthia thought she'd ever do with her best friend, but she was comforted by the thought she wasn't alone.

"The email subject line said, 'this could be you,' and in the body of the email, it tells me to back off the Cooper Downs case. There's a video. I've never seen anything like it." She couldn't take her eyes off the paused video though she wanted to look away. "It's awful. It shows some asshole about to rape a woman. But not just any woman. I think it might be Jane Doe."

"What do you mean, Jane Doe?" Linda's words sounded fuzzy in Cynthia's head. "From the roof of Ben's building?" Linda asked. Hearing Ben's name helped Cynthia focus.

"Yes! It looks like the video was shot by a third person. They were pretty careful not to show anything that would give away any telling details. They're definitely on a roof. I'm not sure if it's Ben's building though. I've never been up there." Cynthia wanted to call Ben and tell him what was going on.

"I can't believe they would be so stupid, filming that. They're just as good as caught now. If Hack can't figure it out, I've got a great tech guy at the station who could probably trace it."

"Hack will figure it out. He's the best." Cynthia tried to reassure herself, remembering the conversation she'd had with Hack yesterday. "There's no sound, but dammit, I can't stop thinking about that woman. She looks so familiar." Cynthia said, grabbing Maris's journal and using it to fan herself. "You up for some company? I need to get out of here."

"Only if you bring that video with you. And hurry the fuck up! My reporter brain needs a fix."

"Okay, okay." She was happy to hear Linda sounding like her old self, trucker mouth and all. She knew her friend was going to be just fine.

"You know I'm going to blame you if Randy finds out, right?"

"Wouldn't have it any other way, my friend," said Linda.

Cynthia headed to Hack's desk to give him a heads up regarding what she'd just forwarded to him.

"Back so soon, doll?"

Cynthia had no time for friendly chit-chat this time.

"I need a trace on something."

"Wow, you sure been busy, doll." The doll bit was getting old.

"I just forwarded an email to you. I need to know who sent it and if there's any way you can enhance the video. I'd like to know who the asshole is that's starring in it."

"Wow, doll. You're starting to sound like one of the guys. I've never heard you talk like that before. I like it." Hack gave Cynthia a nod of approval.

Cynthia rolled her eyes. "Wait till you see the video, *doll*," she said. She didn't wait for a follow-up retort before adding, "Make sure you copy Randy with anything you find out."

"You got it."

29

When Cynthia arrived at the hospital, Linda was just finishing a donut—maple glazed, Ben's favourite. She looked up to see Cynthia at her door and grinned sheepishly while licking her fingers.

"Don't tell the nurses. They'll be pissed."

Cynthia let out a quick huff and said, "You know they have those rules to help you get better faster, right?"

"Oh please, I'm fine. Well, aside from not remembering anything from our night out and the things I told you earlier. Other than that, I'm fine. What's going on with you and Ben? You just missed him."

"Really?" Cynthia arched her eyebrows then frowned. "You didn't tell him about the death threat, did you?" She walked to the edge of Linda's bed then sat down.

"Seriously? I may have a head injury, but my reporter's instincts are still intact. He just brought me a little treat." Cynthia would have a chat with him later about aiding and abetting hospital patients.

Linda looked down at her bedside tray at the empty Tim Horton's bag. "Said he was checking up on me."

"Right. I don't believe you. We made up by the way . . . through voicemail. We just keep missing each other." She really wanted to call him and tell him about the lead on the Jane Doe case.

"Did you bring the video?"

"Of course." Cynthia pulled out her phone, found her email app, and cued the video attached to the email that said, "This could be you".

When Linda saw the woman on the screen, she snatched

Cynthia's phone.

"You know why you recognize her?" Her gaze met Cynthia's blank expression. "That's Maris Kane, Cyn!"

"What? Are you sure?" Cynthia leaned closer to the phone.

"Absolutely. I've been looking at that woman's face for weeks following her case. Ignore the hair, she's dyed it and cut it. She's also wearing a lot of makeup."

"And she's naked. It feels so wrong watching this."

"Look at her eyes. Ignore the makeup." Both women froze, gawking at the tiny cellphone screen.

"Wait! I know that woman. How did I not see that before?"

"Duh, that's what I just said," replied Linda.

"No, I mean, I met this woman at Ben's that night. I never got her name, but she helped me with the elevator when my hands were full of Chinese food."

Linda turned her head so she could see Cynthia's eyes.

"So that was Maris." Cynthia said disheartened. They watched the rest of the video and saw Maris go flying to her death over the edge of Ben's building. "Jesus. Her poor mom will be devastated," Cynthia said.

"Wait," Linda said as Cynthia reached for the home-screen button on her phone. "Play it again."

"What is it?" Cynthia knew Linda better than anyone, and she could tell when she was onto something. She set up the video and watched Linda intently while she viewed the video wide-eyed, not daring to make a move. Cynthia saw a flicker of something on Linda's face. It was a look she'd never seen before.

Linda turned to Cynthia and whispered, "That's my attacker."

"What?! Are you sure?" Cynthia's mouth gaped while she waited for Linda to respond.

"It's hard to trust myself with this foggy, drugged-up head, but I'm pretty sure. I remember seeing a gloved hand coming straight at my face. He placed one hand on the roof of my car as if to stop me from pushing past him. I remember seeing yellow. Look." Linda backed up the video and paused it so Cynthia could see what she was talking about. It was too blurry and small to tell what it was, other than yellow, but there it was on the glove holding the gun.

"I'll see if Hack can blow that up. Maybe give us a clue." Cynthia turned off her phone and tucked it back in her bag.

"There's something I've been meaning to ask you," Cynthia said, turning back to her friend. "Why did you go to your car that night?"

Linda looked at Cynthia, a blank expression on her face. "I don't know. I would never ditch you. Unless . . ."

Cynthia frowned, feeling a little hurt.

"No," Linda continued. "Even if it was a story emergency, I would have told you." She touched her fingers to her throbbing head. "I wish I could remember, Cyn. I'm sorry."

Cynthia shrugged and gestured with her hand, indicating it was no big deal.

"Did Randy come and take your statement yet?" she asked.

"Yesterday. Not that long after I woke up. I was still pretty out of it. I better call him and find out if there was anything else he wanted to ask."

"I don't get it. Randy assured me Jane Doe wasn't Maris. The Medical Examiner's report should have proven she was. Either Randy was lying to me, or the report's wrong. That's clearly Maris Kane on that roof."

"Why would Randy lie to you?"

"I don't know. Something's felt off about this case from the beginning. Why would he want me helping out on a missing person's case? I find missing numbers, not missing people."

"Maybe he recognized your investigative skills. Not everyone knows the right questions to ask. I see that all the time in reporting."

"I hope you're right." Cynthia stood from where she'd been sitting on the edge of Linda's bed, not wanting to face the possibility Randy had been lying to her.

"You're not leaving already, are you? I'm dying of boredom in here." Linda reached for Cynthia's arm like a toddler pleading for their parent to stay.

Cynthia smiled. "Yeah, I know how well you deal with boredom, but I need to figure out what's going on. I'd like to take a look at the ME's report and show Randy the video. He needs to switch his focus from looking for Maris to solving her murder. Maybe we'll get your attacker at the same time."

"Be careful. I don't want you ending up in here too—"

"Hey," Cynthia interrupted. "Are you still dating Troy at the ME's office? Maybe I could ask him for a copy of the report and see the proof for myself that it was Maris on the roof."

"Uh . . ." Linda grimaced. "Troy's a little upset with me right now."

Cynthia rolled her eyes, knowing what Linda was like with men. "What'd you do?"

"He may have seen me out with someone else."

"Oh boy. So, no favours from Troy."

"Sorry, Cyn."

"No worries. I'll find another way." Cynthia took a few more steps in the direction of the hall then swore under her breath. "Dammit."

"What?"

"I forgot to ask Randy what I need to do to get a gun this morning. I'm pretty sure it's not that easy since I work in the office, but I thought it might be worth a try. I could use some extra protection."

"It's not like having a gun would have helped me the other night. I never saw that guy coming. You got pepper spray?"

"In my purse." She tapped her bag, indicating it was safely tucked away. She ran back to Linda's bedside and gave her a goodbye squeeze. "See you soon." She turned and hurried out the door, planning her next move.

30

As Cynthia passed the waiting area, she heard a familiar voice call her name. She turned in the direction she'd come from and saw Ben standing in the hall with a bouquet of white and yellow roses. She inhaled their fresh scent as she walked towards him.

"Hi, stranger," she said, giving him a hug, being careful not to squish the bouquet. "Linda said you'd been here earlier. Did you forget to tell her something?" Cynthia looked at the flowers. Were Linda and Ben closer than she knew? She gave her head a shake at the ridiculous thought.

"I have a confession to make," Ben said. Oh no. In her experience, not a single conversation started with a confession had been a good one.

"Every time I've come to see Linda," Ben continued, "I've come hoping to find you. I know how close you two are, and I felt awful about the other night. And then we kept missing each other on the phone. I just wanted to see you." Ben bent his face towards Cynthia's, and their lips met with a soft kiss. "Oh . . . these are for you." He handed Cynthia the roses. Her face flushed.

"Thank you."

"There's something else, but I was hoping we might have a chance to talk in private."

"You know . . ." Cynthia paused, thinking about finding the ME's report on Jane Doe back at the office. "There's something I need to take care of at the police station, but why don't you come with me? We can talk on the way."

"Are you sure? We can meet later."

"I'm sure. You've got me curious now. Plus, I have some news about the woman from your building." Cynthia shot Ben a sideways glance as they headed down the hospital hall, hands interlocked.

Once they were inside Cynthia's Focus, seat belts on and ready to go, Ben grabbed Cynthia's hand before she had a chance to put the car in gear, causing her to stop and look at him. He grabbed her face with both hands and gave her another kiss, this time long and slow. When he was done, Cynthia almost forgot where she was and what she had planned to do. Her eyes locked with Ben's as if they were frozen in time.

"I love you," he said. "I was a jerk before because I didn't know what I was feeling. I'm sorry. I didn't think I would feel so deeply for you so quickly."

"Uh," was all Cynthia managed to squeak out. "I—"

"You don't have to say anything," Ben interrupted. "I just wanted you to know why I've been acting so weird. When that body hit my balcony, it made me realize you just never know what can happen in life, and I freaked out."

"Speaking of the body," Cynthia said, more than happy to change the subject, "You have to watch something. It explains what happened that night, but it's very graphic. Can you handle that?" Cynthia looked at Ben. He nodded as if in slow motion, perhaps trying to brace himself for what he was about to see. She grabbed her purse from the back seat and pulled out her phone. She cued up the video, careful not to let Ben see she'd received it as a death threat. She handed her phone to Ben. "You're not seeing this, understand? This is evidence."

Cynthia had told Ben details of her cases before. Since they were both accountants, it was easy for them to talk about the ways fraudsters tried to steal and hide their money, but this was taking it to a new level.

"Of course," Ben said, pressing play on the video while Cynthia put the car in gear and started in the direction of the station.

Ben sat in silence while he watched then finally said, "This . . . is the worst thing I've ever seen."

"We'll soon know what happened to Maris Kane," said Cynthia.

"That's Maris Kane?"

"Yes. She was clearly hiding from someone the way she had changed her look so dramatically."

"Jesus Christ," Ben said, staring out the window as city lights and storefronts whizzed by.

31

Paul and Kelly followed a few vehicles behind Cynthia and Ben in Vivian's black Camaro.

"Those two lovebirds make me sick," Paul said. "Did you see them in the hospital parking lot?"

Kelly sat motionless.

"I said, did you see them?" he raised his voice and brandished his revolver at Kelly while keeping his other hand on the wheel.

"Yeah, I saw them," Kelly said, her voice soft. "What are we doing, Paul?" She stared out the front windshield while she talked. "I don't understand what good following Cynthia is—"

"Shut up. I never asked for your opinion."

"I—" Kelly tried to explain.

"On any of it," Paul snapped. "I only brought you in for your skills, so keep your trap shut." He jabbed her in the thigh with his gun. Kelly put her elbow on the armrest and hung her head in her hand, staring at the floor.

"Not that it's any of your business," continued Paul, "but this Cynthia bitch needs to learn a lesson."

Kelly lifted her head and took a breath as if she was going to say something, but Paul wouldn't let her get a word in.

"I told her to stay away. But you heard her at the hospital talking to your reporter friend—"

"She's not my friend," Kelly said, her voice barely audible.

"Oh, right, I forgot, you're just a little do-gooder," Paul said, cackling from deep within his gut. "Do-gooder," he said again, nudging Kelly with his elbow. "You like that?"

Kelly turned in her seat to face Paul. "I told you, I don't like people getting hurt. There's no reason for it. My part in this is coding, that's it."

"You'll do what I tell you to do." Paul waved his gun in the air, and Kelly turned back to face the road.

The signal lights on Cynthia's car blinked right, indicating they would be exiting the highway. Paul swerved the Camaro to the right without a signal and barely a shoulder check.

He parked the Camaro and turned off the lights but kept it idling. He could see the police station from where he was parked, but he kept the car out of the station parking lot. Paul watched as Cynthia ran into the station. He put the car in gear and flicked the lights on.

"Looks like it's time for the next stage," he said under his breath.

"The next stage?" Kelly asked. "What's the next stage? The final ticket?"

Paul cackled again. "You'll find out soon enough." He maneuvered the Camaro back onto the highway and headed north. The car lurched forward as Paul stomped on the gas. "Ha, ha, yeah, baby," he said, pounding the steering wheel. Knuckles white, Kelly gripped the holy-shit handle above her head.

When they arrived at the parking lot behind the Cooper Downs stables, Paul cranked the wheel and slammed on the brakes, causing the Camaro to skid to a stop at the darkest edge of the parking lot near a clump of trees behind the stables.

"Get out," Paul said. "It's time to prepare."

Kelly climbed out. "Come on, Paul," she said. "I need to get home. Can't you just tell me what we're doing here?"

Paul shoved Cynthia's business card in Kelly's face. "I know you've been talking to her." Kelly felt the breast pocket of her jean jacket for Cynthia's card. There was nothing there. Her face turned red.

"Fuck you, Paul. Stay out of my stuff."

"You want to help the police catch us?" he asked.

"I never said a word."

"Give me your phone," he said, placing his gun at Kelly's

temple. Kelly reached around to her back pocket and passed her cell to Paul. Keeping his gun trained on Kelly, Paul entered Cynthia's number then sent her a text message.

"What did you say?" Kelly asked.

"Never mind," he said. "You're not gonna like it. People are about to get hurt." He lowered his gun then jerked it up, hitting Kelly in the jaw. She fell sideways and landed flat on her back. Paul kicked her and tossed her phone on her body.

"Stupid, bitch," he said. "Should have done what you were told." He ran to the stables to prepare for his guest.

32

Cynthia felt her stomach rumble as she parked her Focus in her spot at the station. She turned to Ben, thinking about what he'd confessed to her earlier.

"About before. I'm sorry I didn't have a chance to properly respond." She put her hand on Ben's thigh.

"It's okay. I meant it. You don't need to say anything. Actually, I don't want you to say anything." He crossed his arms and turned his nose towards the sky putting on a fake display of indignation. Cynthia laughed and punched him in the shoulder, despite her trepidations about what she was about to do.

"I won't be long. Why don't you hang out here then we can go somewhere and talk? My parents took Luke to the cabin, so I've got all night. We can grab a late dinner."

"Perfect." He winked at her as she got out and closed the door. His winks had always made her feel special, but tonight she barely noticed. She was too busy trying to figure out what to do next.

Cynthia ran into the building, which added to the nerves she was already feeling. It was after hours, so there was nobody at reception. She wasn't sure how she would approach the subject of the ME's report with Randy, and she hoped he may have misread it.

Her purse was still slung over her shoulder when she sat down at her desk to log on to her computer. The fastest way to check the report was to pull it up on the server, but there was nothing where the report should have been. Strange. Reports were logged in by the document creator, which meant Troy would have put it on the system when it was created. Did Randy delete it?

Thinking the report had been misfiled, she opened more directories. As she did, her email notifications popped up. There was one from Hack. She made a mental note to check it before she left and continued looking for the report on Jane Doe. She checked a few days before Maris's death and a few days after. Still nothing. Her stomach felt jittery as alarm bells started going off in her head. Randy probably had it on his desk. It was probably lost in the sea of paperwork. Maybe Troy was waiting for Randy's approval before filing it?

She padded a couple doors down the hallway to Randy's office, looking outside at Ben sitting in her car as she did. He appeared to be looking at his phone.

The papers on Randy's desk were just as she remembered them earlier that day—as if someone had opened a window during a freak windstorm. She had no idea what she was looking for. There had never been a need for her to view the reports from the Medical Examiner's office before. She assumed there would be some sort of letterhead indicating the report came from their office.

Several dirty coffee cups were being used as paperweights. "Gross," Cynthia said to no one.

"Hello, Cynthia."

"Gah!" Cynthia yelled, jumping as she looked up from Randy's desk to find him in the doorway, eyeing her with concern. She suddenly felt like she was violating his personal space—which she was—but hadn't he told her once to make herself at home?

"Hey, Randy. I couldn't find the ME's report on Jane Doe," Cynthia said, pretending not to know about Maris Kane. "I thought it might be in one of your piles of paper. You really need an assistant." Cynthia tried a joke to cover up her nervousness, but she got no response from Randy. His usual jovial demeanour was gone. She looked up to find a blank stare on his face.

"What do you need the report for?"

All the moisture in Cynthia's mouth had disappeared. She struggled to swallow.

"I . . . uh . . . wanted to double-check the date and time of death."

"I thought you had a photographic memory for dates?" Randy had her there. She gulped some air.

"It's for Ben," she lied. "I thought if he knew the exact time of death, it might help him forget about that night." Oh shit. Her words sounded pathetic even to her. There's no way Randy would buy it. She debated telling him Ben was waiting for her, but not sure what Randy was up to, she opted to protect Ben instead. Just stay in the car, she thought, wishing he could read her mind.

"I was hoping it wouldn't come to this," he said with a sigh.

"Come to what?" Cynthia asked.

"Oh, come on." Randy's voice got louder as he stepped closer. "Don't play dumb with me. I meant what I said about your instincts."

Cynthia stepped closer to Randy.

"You're right," she said. "I should be focusing on Maris's case, not trying to help Ben feel better. I'm sorry, Randy," she said, trying to make it seem like she didn't know what was going on. She'd have to come back and snoop through Randy's office another time. She took a few steps towards Randy, and he moved to block the door.

Cynthia felt her heart pounding in her throat. She focused on her breath, while trying hard not to break eye contact with Randy.

She watched him reach behind his back. When his hand returned to where she could see it, she nearly stopped breathing.

33

Randy couldn't believe it had come to this. What the hell was he doing? All he could think about was Vivian and the money she'd promised him. He thought he'd figured out a way to get the money and put Vivian away too, but Cynthia had to back off. He pulled a gun from behind his back and pointed it at her.

"You knew, didn't you?" Cynthia asked, taking a few steps back. "You knew all along, and you didn't say anything. Why? Why didn't you tell me Jane Doe is Maris Kane? Do you know how much pain and heartache you could have saved?" Too many questions. She was babbling, trying to buy time. He saw perps do this all the time.

"Her poor mother is still holding out hope we'll call her with the good news we've found her daughter and it's safe for her to come out of hiding," Cynthia said.

"I didn't think you'd put it together," Randy said. "I thought you'd be so busy with the fraud case. But, I guess I have Paul to thank for your little discovery. He just loves to threaten people. I'm sorry about that." The confusion on Cynthia's face seemed to grow. "I saw the video he sent you," Randy explained. "And I'm sorry about this too." He waved his gun. "But I can't have you expose this. Maris needs to stay missing," he said.

"Why? I don't understand. Who's Paul?" Cynthia's eyes widened as if she realized what Randy was implying. Was she playing with him?

"Paul, from Maris's journal," Randy said, standing steadfast in the doorway, his gun still trained on Cynthia.

With narrowed eyes and pursed lips, Cynthia said, "You knew

it was Paul who killed Maris?" Cynthia gulped some air and looked from side to side. "What's going on, Randy? Whatever it is, let me help. So you made a mistake. We can fix it."

Randy shook his head. "There's no way out, Cynthia. I'm in too deep. I shouldn't have let this go on for so long. Vivian has me by the short hairs. There's nothing I can do if I want to keep working as a detective. My career is as good as over." As the words came out of his mouth, Randy knew what he needed to do was come clean, but he feared it was too late for that. He hoped he could at least take Vivian down with him.

"Please, let me help you." Cynthia started to walk towards him again.

"Stay back," he said. He really didn't want to shoot her, but he didn't want her ruining his career either. Sweat was starting to bead at his brows. He used the back of his hand to wipe it away.

"I know you're not a bad person," she said. "This isn't you. Something else is going on." She'd gotten that right.

"Don't come any closer." Randy jutted the pistol towards Cynthia as the tension rose in his body. She was close enough to him now that the gun almost touched her. "Don't force me to use this on you." His voice cracked as he met Cynthia's gaze.

A distant banging caused Randy to step out of the doorway and glance down the hall. He looked back at Cynthia. "Who's here with you?" he asked, concern and anger on his face.

"Nobody. I'm alone," she said. "It's probably just the night guard." Randy didn't buy it. Her tone was similar to a criminal's when they lied to cover up for their buddies.

"Come on, Randy, don't throw away your whole career for this. We can still make this right," she said. He wanted to believe her. Oh, how he wanted to believe her.

His muscles relaxed and he lowered his gun slightly. Could she really help him? He left the gun pointed at the ground, but kept his gaze trained on hers, not totally trusting there was a way out of this yet.

He took a step backwards into the hall as he threw up his

arms. "It's too late. I fucked up. I'm screwed no matter what." He pointed the gun at the floor again and contemplated taking his own life. But what about Kat? What about Boo?

"You're smarter than this," Cynthia interrupted his thoughts. "Take the high road and come clean. I know that's what you want to do. What would Kat think of this?" she asked.

The mention of Kat's name shocked Randy. How did Cynthia know how much Kat meant to him? He searched his memory and his muscles relaxed a bit.

She was right, he did want to come clean. Kat had encouraged him to do the same thing.

"Cynthia . . ." He inhaled deeply, preparing to bombard her with all the sordid details of his desperate financial affairs. "You're right. I do." He wiped his brow with the back of the hand holding the gun then put his arm to the side, preparing to tuck his gun back into its holster, but before his gun was tucked away where it should be, someone flew at him from the side and knocked him to the floor.

He heard a panicked voice he recognized, yelling in his ear. "Cynthia, run! Get the guard!" the voice echoed.

34

Cynthia ran to the hallway to find Randy and Ben rolling around on the floor. "No, Ben!" she screamed. "Stop!" She couldn't catch her breath. She wanted to tell him everything was okay, that she was handling it, but panic took over. All she could manage to say was "stop" again.

"Ben, please, stop!"

But he wasn't giving up. The two men were grunting and scrambling, their limbs entwined. Her yelling was useless.

She ran down the hall, yelling for whoever was on duty. "Help! Come quick! It's Detective Bain." She met up with Officer Scott. He was already running towards her.

"What's going on?"

"Detective Bain needs help. He says he fucked up." Warren frowned at Cynthia. "I have no idea what he's talking about. He pulled his gun on me. Then he was going to tell me everything, but my boyfriend attacked him."

"Jesus," said Warren, running with Cynthia down the hall. Before they got to where Ben and Randy were struggling, a deafening shot rang out, causing Cynthia to go numb. She gasped for breath at what she saw in front of her. Ben and Randy were in a heap on the floor, but she couldn't tell if either one was hurt. Randy struggled to get himself free from beneath Ben.

As Cynthia knelt beside the men, Randy managed to roll Ben off him. Ben flopped lifelessly to Randy's side, a large pool of blood seeping through his shirt.

"No!" Cynthia screamed. She wanted to shove Randy out of the way, but he was already checking for Ben's pulse. Then he started CPR.

"What have you done?" She looked at Randy with tears in her eyes, Ben between them. "Ben! Come on, Ben! You're going to be okay!" she yelled. There was no response from Ben as Cynthia grabbed his hand.

"Warren, call 911!" Randy yelled. "It was an accident." Randy was crying now too as he continued to work on Ben. "Why'd you have to go and be all heroic?" he sputtered through intermittent sobs. His face was soaked with sweat and tears.

Warren did as Randy asked then reported back. "The EMTs are on their way." He knelt beside Cynthia. "Why don't you make room for the EMTs."

"No!" Cynthia snapped at Warren. "I'm not leaving him." This can't be happening. "Come on, Ben." She shook his hand a little. Sirens blared in the background as tears fell from her cheeks and mixed with the blood on Ben's shirt. She wiped her nose with her sleeve.

When she looked up, she saw ambulance lights in the parking lot. Soon after, the EMTs ran down the hallway with a gurney. Randy refused to stop CPR.

"Come on." Warren placed his hands on Randy's shoulders. "Let them do their job," he said as he pried Randy off Ben. "I'm sorry, man," Warren said, "but until I find out what happened here, I'm going to—"

"I know the drill." Randy cut him off. "You have to lock me up."

The EMTs made quick work of getting Ben on the gurney.

"Ben," Cynthia said in Ben's ear as the EMTs wheeled him away. "I love you . . ." her voice trailed off as she stared down the hall, watching the EMTs do their job. One continued CPR while two others directed the gurney.

From the hallway, she watched out the window as the EMTs loaded Ben into the ambulance, lights still flashing. The siren blared again. Cynthia stayed frozen in place until the ambulance had disappeared out of her line of sight. As if all the energy had drained out of her body, she braced herself against the wall then slumped down to the floor. She sat there, eyes wide, staring straight ahead.

35

It had been about ten minutes since the EMTs had left with
Ben, and Cynthia hadn't moved from the bloody spot in the
hallway. She sat there staring, too shocked to cry. Not since Jason
had died had she felt so empty.

"Cynthia?" Warren sat beside her and gently put his hand on
her shoulder. "Is there anyone I can call for you?" No response.
He waited a minute or two, sitting and staring, then tried again.
"Do you need a ride to the hospital?"

Warren's mention of the word "hospital" triggered a memory of
the day Jason had died. She'd rushed to the hospital when she'd
gotten the call he'd been in an accident. She thought if she could
get there quickly, he'd be okay. But she'd arrived at the hospital
only to learn he'd died instantly at the accident scene. No, going
to the hospital wasn't what she wanted to do right now.

"No . . ." She looked at Warren. "I . . . I'll be all right." She
thought about Ryan, Ben's best friend, whom they had both
worked with at D&A. He'd want to know Ben had been taken
to the hospital. She should call him.

"I need to call Ben's friend." Warren stood and offered his
hand to Cynthia. "The ambulance left with sirens blazing and
lights flashing. That's good, right?" she asked Warren, reaching
for his hand.

Warren pulled Cynthia to her feet. "I'm sure it is." He smiled
a half-hearted smile but wasn't very convincing. "You want a
coffee?" he asked.

"No, thank you." She felt a little queasy. "I'm a tea drinker,"
she added, unsure why that mattered right now. "I don't need
anything, thanks. I'm just going to take a breather in my office

then I'll head to the hospital." She knew that was a lie. The last place she wanted to be was the hospital. The last thing she wanted to hear were the words, "I'm sorry, there was nothing we could do." She'd avoid that as long as possible. Maybe if Ryan went, Ben would be okay. Yes, she had to call Ryan.

"All right," Warren said. "I'm here all night. I'll need your statement when you're ready to talk about what happened. Then I'm happy to take you to the hospital." Warren left Cynthia in her office. As she sat at her desk, she felt bile creeping up her throat and she swallowed hard. Her face flushed, and she placed her hands on her desk to help the dizziness pass.

She slumped down in her chair, took a deep breath, and dialed Ben's best friend, Ryan. He was really the only friend of Ben's she knew, and because she'd worked with him on her last audit file at D&A, she had his number. Ryan was stunned and planned to head straight to the hospital. He said he'd see her there. She wanted to add, "I'm not sure you will," but she knew she'd end up there eventually.

"Why?!" she cried out. "Why?" Frantic sobs took over her body, and she folded her arms on her desk and put her head down and bawled into them. She bawled for Ben, but she also bawled for Jason.

Warren brought her a bottle of water. She sobbed for a few more minutes, and Warren gave her some privacy. She wanted to go to the hospital but felt stuck in her chair. Maybe after she told Warren what had happened, she'd be ready for that ride. She just needed a bit more time to collect herself before she went to find Warren.

She looked to her laptop for a distraction. While wiping her eyes with a Kleenex, she opened the email she'd seen earlier from Hack, hoping for some sort of good news on the Cooper Downs case. It appeared as if someone had hacked into the Cooper Downs network to print the tickets on their printer, which meant, in Hack's opinion, there was a good chance Cynthia was looking for a partnership. A programmer and someone on the inside. Whoever had hacked into the Cooper Downs network knew how to cover their tracks and had masked their IP address, but Hack was pretty sure he'd have it figured out by morning.

This break in the case should have made Cynthia feel better, but she couldn't get Ben out of her head. She needed to get to the hospital, but she was afraid of losing someone else. What would she tell Luke? She put her elbows on her desk and covered her face with her hands then took a deep breath and waited for the room to stop spinning. Her cell pinged from inside her purse, which she'd left strewn across her desk when she'd gone to search Randy's office for the ME's report.

She pulled out her phone. It was a number she didn't recognize, but she saw the first part of the message, and her heartbeat thrashed in her ears. No, it couldn't be. She swiped up and clicked through to the rest of the message.

We have your son. Cooper Downs stable. No cops. Come now.

It couldn't be. Luke was safe with Mom and Dad. Again, bile rose to her throat. She swiped to the call app, found the entry marked "Cabin" in her contacts, and pressed the call button. It went straight to voicemail. Jesus.

"Mom, call me as soon as you get this. It's an emergency." Shit, shit, shit! She stood and took a wobbly step back as she tried to steady herself. Get a grip, Cynthia.

Her next thought was to get Warren. "No cops," rang in her head. In desperation, she ran to the basement where they kept all the drugs and weapons seized during arrests. It was locked. Of course. Should have asked for a goddamn gun. Warren met Cynthia on her way back upstairs. She rushed past him.

"Everything okay?" he asked.

"No," she said with clenched teeth. "I'm going to the hospital," she lied, hoping he'd stay put. She had to get Luke back, but how was she going to do that without Warren's help? Adrenaline kicked in, and the weakness and nausea she'd felt earlier was replaced with rage and sheer determination.

Once in her car, the fragrant smell of roses coming from the backseat pulled her attention back to Ben for a second. She couldn't think about him right now. She needed to hurry if she was going to save Luke, so she chose the fastest route she knew that went north to the racetrack. She prayed a plan would come to her on the drive. She tried the cabin again—voicemail. Why wasn't Mom answering her phone? Did they have her too?

The thought of Luke tied up somewhere made her hysterical, but that wasn't going to do anyone any good. She shook her head, trying to rid it of the unwelcome image. Hang on, baby, Mama's coming.

36

When she arrived at Cooper Downs, Cynthia parked in the casino parking lot and walked towards the stables on what seemed like a service road. It was dark, and she hoped she could sneak up to the stables, assess the situation, and come up with a plan to get Luke back.

There were no races coming up, which meant even though the stables sometimes boarded horses, they would be fairly quiet. Why would the kidnappers want to meet here? Then it dawned on her. Hack had mentioned a partnership. The ticket fraud had to be an inside job.

Kelly, the woman who had let her out of Vivian's office, had said she was a groomer. Was she the one who'd texted her? It didn't make sense to Cynthia that she would be involved somehow. If she was involved, why free her from Vivian's office?

Cynthia snuck up to the window closest to the north entrance of the stables. She peered in, looking for any sign of Luke. Nothing. She'd have to sneak alongside the building to the other entrance and see if Luke was there. A chill came over her and she reached in her purse for the pepper spray. As she turned to check over her shoulder—

Smack!

Then darkness as she toppled to the grass, the pepper spray landing beside her.

***

A gentle vibration and light whirring noise stirred Cynthia from unconsciousness. She opened her eyes and felt her lashes brush against the rough fabric covering her head. Some sort of bag? She tried to sit up, but her hands were bound together. Her wrists felt sticky—duct tape. She let out a scream that forced all the air out of her lungs in a long sharp burst.

"Shut up, bitch. Nobody here but you and me."

That voice. She knew that voice. The gentle purring of an engine and the jerky stops and starts told her she was riding in a vehicle—in the city.

"Where's Luke?"

"Never mind about him right now. I thought you wanted to know about Maris Kane. That's what's gotten you into this mess, isn't it? I tried to warn you this would happen."

The image of the death threat and its video contents came soaring back to her. She sucked in a quick gasp then sputtered as fabric from the bag caught in her mouth.

"You sent the video? Did you do that to her?"

It was sweltering inside the bag. She could feel moisture starting to form at her hair line. Her head throbbed.

"You'll find out soon enough. Now, shut your trap or I might change my mind."

Cynthia closed her eyes. There was no use keeping them open. Having her head covered made her feel like she was in a tunnel. She willed her other senses to work. Her mouth was dry, and she could feel acid rising in the back of her throat. Keep it together, Cynthia.

She took a deep breath to calm her nerves but inhaled more fabric instead, which only caused her to panic more. She spit it out, and bits of burlap stuck to her tongue. Tears trickled down her face, and she let out a whimper.

"I said, shut up!" came the voice from the front. Her hair felt hot and damp on the side of her head at the site of the searing pain. The vehicle slowed and turned to the left. It felt as if it went down a short ramp then turned to the right. Another right and then it came to a stop.

The driver got out and opened the door closest to Cynthia.

He grabbed her by the shoulders so she was sitting up in the vehicle. He tugged at the casing around her head until she was exposed to the light. She gasped for air and blinked several times in reaction to the bright light in the parking garage. As her eyes adjusted, the man holding her in place came into focus. He wore a uniform with a name tag. "Paul". Confirmation of his guilt meant nothing right now. The blade of a knife glinted in front of her face.

"Where's Luke? What do you want with me?" She tried to steady her voice and took another jerky breath.

"I told you to shut up."

He shoved the knife closer to her face then forced her hands to the side. He used the knife to remove the duct tape holding her hands together. He grabbed her by her wrist and yanked her out of the vehicle. She narrowly missed hitting her head on the door frame. Cynthia looked around, taking in as much of her surroundings as possible.

The vehicle she now stood beside was a newer black sports car made to look like a classic. She thought it might be a Camaro, but without a reference photo to compare to, she wasn't totally sure. She quickly scanned beyond the vehicle and realized they were in a parking garage. One she'd been in many times before.

37

As if sensing her recognition of the parking garage, Paul said, "You try anything funny, and all I have to do is make one phone call and your son is dead." He lifted his shirt to expose the gun in his waistband and put the knife back into its sheath on his belt.

Cynthia couldn't help thinking about Ben as she looked around the parking garage of his building. She saw the empty parking spot where his car would normally be parked and swallowed hard, trying not to think about whether or not he was alive. A tear trickled down her cheek. She should be at the hospital. Ryan was waiting for her, but Luke was more important that any of that. Where the hell was he? What did Paul want? She had to think quick. Get him talking.

"How do I know you haven't already killed him?" She braced herself for Paul's response.

"I guess you'll just have to trust me," he said.

Right. Because you've done so much to earn my trust already, Cynthia thought but didn't dare retaliate. She thought back to yesterday when she'd run into Paul at Cooper Downs. She'd had a bad feeling about him then. Was her running into him an accident? Why were they here? Did Paul and Ben know each other?

Paul jerked Cynthia from her thoughts when he grabbed one of her elbows and shoved her in front of him, guiding her towards the service elevator. When they got in, Paul pressed "PH" for the penthouse. How would Paul explain himself if anyone joined them in the elevator? She prayed the elevator stopped before Paul's requested floor. Paul held Cynthia's arm tight the entire ride up, his fingers digging into her skin. When the elevator came to a sudden stop at the penthouse, Cynthia felt her stomach lurch into her chest.

The elevator doors opened into the hallway. Along the hall were two doors, one on each side. Paul unlocked the door to the apartment on the left. Cynthia could hardly believe her eyes. Fresh tulips filled a glass vase on the kitchen island, and pristine white furniture accented the living room beyond the kitchen. Such a peaceful-looking apartment. It was hard to imagine Paul living here. A table was adorned with two place settings, and an open bottle of champagne sat in the middle of the table. A champagne glass sat to the side of each place setting—champagne already poured.

Ding.

Something made a noise in the kitchen, and Cynthia jumped then tried to break free from the death grip Paul had on her arm.

"I told you not to try anything funny," Paul said, sticking his pointer finger in Cynthia's face. "I need to check on dinner. You wait right here and enjoy some champagne." He forced her to sit in one of the chairs at the table. The sarcasm in his voice was all the warning Cynthia needed not to touch the sweet liquid.

She looked around the apartment for a weapon or a means of escape while Paul took something that looked like a roast out of the oven. The butt of his gun stuck out of his waistband when he bent over.

Cynthia found it odd that everything in the apartment made it feel like a woman lived there. The artwork, the furniture, how neat and tidy it was. The walls were filled with photographs of horses and jockeys, much like Vivian's office. A familiar purple trench coat hung on the back of one of the chairs at the kitchen island. Cynthia remembered the smell of Chinese food as the image of the man and woman walking in front of her on the way to Ben's apartment flashed in her mind—Paul and Vivian.

"What's going on, Paul?" She risked another question. Paul slammed his fist on the cutting board he'd been using to slice the roast, carving knife still in hand. Cynthia sat up poker straight in her chair.

"Damn it! I already told you," he said, turning to face Cynthia. "You want to know what happened to Maris so badly? Well, you're going to find out. I'm going to show you every little detail."

Paul stomped in Cynthia's direction, making it to the table in just a few strides. He held the carving knife up to her chin. "But . . . you need . . . to shut . . . your trap." He used the knife to lift Cynthia's chin, so she was facing him. She made eye contact, afraid to look anywhere else. Then he flicked the knife so it nicked her, and she tightened her lips to keep from making a sound.

"Unfortunately, my mother couldn't make it tonight." It *had been* Paul and Vivian that night. Cynthia remembered a page in Maris's journal, the last entry. Vivian had wanted her to come over for dinner, so they could discuss a plan for her to come back to work. Maris wrote about how she hadn't understood how that was going to work since she was pretty sure it was Paul who had been stalking her. He was the reason she'd been hiding out for the last two weeks.

"Oh, I almost forgot," Paul said, "grab your plate. We're going upstairs."

Cynthia's muscles tightened and her heart raced. The only upstairs from the penthouse was the roof.

38

Cynthia sat across from Paul at a table on the roof of Ben's apartment building.

"That's more like it," he said, taking a bite of the roast. "This is where Mom and Maris were when I found them. Mom made me stay out of sight. She told me she was going to *handle* Maris and her meddling, but it was taking too long. When I came up here, they were laughing and joking like two best friends."

There were many questions Cynthia wanted to ask, but she thought about Luke and chose to remain silent as Paul had warned her. She looked around while Paul ate the dinner that had been mysteriously cooked for them. After surveying the rooftop with as much discretion as she could, Cynthia caught Paul's eye.

"Not hungry?" he asked. Cynthia shrugged her shoulders. How could she possibly eat when she had no idea where Luke was or what Paul was going to do with her? She picked up her knife and fork, hoping to convince Paul she would eat so she could continue to observe her surroundings.

Other than smacking him over the head with her plate and making a run for the door they'd arrived through, she had no idea how she was going to save herself. Paul's phone sat on the table. She'd need that too if she was going to find out who had Luke and where they were.

That's what she'd do. It was her only option—wait until Paul was distracted, then hit him with as much force as she could manage, steal his phone, and make a run for it. She hoped the plate was heavy enough to get the job done. Her stomach flip-flopped at the thought of food filling it, but she'd have to play along if she was going to have any chance at saving herself and Luke. She took her fork and fluffed up the mashed potatoes that sat beside the slice of roast on her plate. As she lifted the fork towards her mouth, she raised her gaze slightly. Paul glanced at his phone, and with the speed and swiftness of a highly trained martial artist karate-chopping a block of wood, she grabbed her plate with both hands and swung at his face as hard as she could and took off running, not stopping to look back.

"You ungrateful little bitch," she heard from behind her. "I cook you dinner and you treat me like this." The sound of Paul standing and pushing his chair back sounded like fingernails scraping a chalkboard.

"You know, Maris tried the same thing. This is going well," he said. "Exactly as planned."

Cynthia didn't stop or turn around. She kept sprinting for the door. Just as she grabbed the knob, she looked behind to see Paul was just standing there watching her, smiling. Something was wrong. She tried the door. It was locked. Shit.

Hysterical laughing came from the madman behind her. "You're mine now," he said with an evil snicker. Cynthia ran in the direction of the railing furthest from Paul and looked over, hoping to find a fire escape ladder. Something. Anything.

"Time for the main event," he said, pulling his gun from his waistband and walking towards Cynthia. He towered over her. She knew he would outpace her five-foot frame if she tried to run. She darted to her left anyway. With one swift leap, Paul lunged at her and grabbed on. As she fell, Cynthia let out such a high-pitched, gut-wrenching scream she felt a pop in one of her ears and her throat throbbed.

Paul shoved his gun so hard into her cheek between her teeth, she thought it was going to poke through to the inside of her mouth. He dragged her to a spot against the railing as she tried to kick herself free.

"I think you know what happens now," he said. With horror, Cynthia thought back to the image on the video, Maris's naked body flying off the balcony.

"Take off your clothes," said Paul.

39

Cynthia was pinned against the railing almost directly across from the access door. Paul took two steps back from Cynthia and she took the opportunity to exhale.

He pointed the gun at her face. She wondered what he considered the main event to be. Was he going to rape her? Kill her? He had clearly intended to rape Maris on the video. Cynthia hoped rape was his end game rather than murder. If that was the case, she could throw off his plan by not doing what he asked.

"Did you hear me? I said, take off your clothes."

Cynthia stared so intently at Paul that everything else around her became a blur.

"You want me to take off my clothes, then you're going to have to give me what I want. I need to know where my son is."

Paul took a step closer to Cynthia and touched the gun to her forehead. "You're just going to have to trust me."

"Trust? You know nothing about trust, asshole. You kidnap my son, and you want me to trust you?"

"I don't see how you have much choice, bitch. I'm the one holding the gun." Paul pressed the gun harder into her forehead and gave it a little twist.

"Without my son, I might as well be dead. Go ahead and shoot me." Cynthia was eerily calm, a drastic change from only minutes ago. She meant what she'd said. Luke was her life. Paul took a step back, again, as if he was surprised by her refusal to do as he'd asked. He looked as if he was contemplating his next move when the door opened behind him.

Cynthia hoped he hadn't heard the door and maintained eye contact with him, imagining she was searing through his skull with her eyes. She was too scared to look beyond Paul and see who had joined them on the rooftop, but since they weren't making any noise, she guessed they were either too scared or they were expecting to find the scene they'd stumbled upon. Her grip on the railing behind her tightened as she prepared for the worst.

"Put down your weapon," came Officer Scott's voice from behind Paul. Paul turned to look at Warren, and Cynthia took the opportunity to bolt for the door and the woman standing there. It was Kelly.

"Don't close the door," Cynthia said, "it will lock behind you." Kelly stuck her foot in front of the door, preventing it from closing. She had a strange expression on her face Cynthia couldn't read.

"Put down your weapon," Warren said again.

Both women looked towards the railing. Sirens blared in the distance, and familiar red and blue flashing lights reflected off the glass of neighbouring apartment buildings. "Come on, man. This could end very badly for you if you don't put down your weapon *right now.*" Officer Scott seemed determined to defuse the situation.

"Fuck you, cop!" Paul flew at Warren and a shot rang out. Both men were knocked to the ground. Paul's gun slid straight at the women, and Cynthia snatched it up and pointed it at Paul.

"Stop!" she said as loudly as she could. "Where's my son?" She jabbed the gun in Paul's direction while walking towards him.

Both men, now on their feet, stopped and looked towards Cynthia.

"Fuck you, bitch," said Paul.

Cynthia continued marching directly at Paul, his own gun still pointed at him. Blood leaked through his shirt just below his collar bone.

"Cynthia, I've got this," Warren said, also pointing his gun at Paul. "Don't do anything stupid."

Cynthia ignored Warren, her eyes still focused on Paul. "I said, where's my son, *bitch?*"

In one swift motion, Paul whipped out his knife and thrust it at Cynthia. She pulled the trigger, and Paul fell backwards. A pool of blood seeped out from under his body. Cynthia dropped the gun, and Warren ran over to her.

"If you hadn't done it, I would have," he said. "We did all we could to calm him. He would have killed you."

Cynthia's hand flew to her mouth at the thought that she'd just killed the only person who knew where Luke was.

40

Cynthia sat alone at one of the tables on the rooftop watching officers process the table where she'd sat across from Paul. After answering several questions from one of the officers, a paramedic gave Cynthia a blanket and some water, checked her over, and found nothing requiring medical attention besides the bump on the forehead she'd sustained when Paul had kidnapped her.

The paramedic recommended she go to the hospital, and she promised she would get one of the officers to drop her off when they found Luke. The thought of going to the hospital made her throat constrict, and she wondered if Warren knew if Ben was alive. Kelly approached Cynthia, closely followed by one of the officers.

"I heard you mention your son," she said. "I don't know where he is, but I do know Paul didn't take him. He threatened me and took my phone so it would look like I texted you that message. I'm so sorry. He never had him." Her eyes were glassy. She looked away from Cynthia then back again. "I'm so sorry," she repeated.

Cynthia looked up, hope in her eyes. "Luke's safe?" she asked. Kelly nodded. Cynthia's shoulders dropped as she relaxed a little. "Why wouldn't he just text me himself? I don't know either of your numbers."

"That was Paul. He always had to feel like a big man ordering people around. He knew I let you out of Vivian's office yesterday. I'm pretty sure he was the one who locked you in there. I had no idea what he was planning to do. I thought he just wanted to scare you."

"Thank you, Kelly. I know you didn't mean any harm." Cynthia looked past Kelly. She needed to hear Luke's voice. Directing her question at the officer standing behind Kelly, she asked, "Do you have a phone I can borrow?"

"Here, take mine," Kelly said, handing her phone to Cynthia. She dialed Mom at the cabin.

A confused "hello" came from the other end.

"It's me, Mom."

"Cynthia. What's going on?"

Cynthia took a breath to answer but Mom wouldn't let her. "You had me worried sick with all your talk about an emergency." Although Cynthia's ears were still ringing from the gunshots, she had to hold Kelly's phone away from her ear to compensate for Mom's shrieking. "I called you four times!"

"Ben's been shot." Might as well give her something to shriek about. She wasn't sure if leading with Ben's story was the best way to go, but it was all that occupied her mind now that she knew Luke was safe.

"My god." She heard Mom gasp on the other end of the phone. "Is he all right?"

"I'm heading to the hospital to find out."

"Should we meet you there?"

"No." That was all she needed—Mom flying to the hospital in panic mode.

"Mom, I really need to talk to Luke. Can you put him on?"

"Of course." Cynthia heard static-like noises as if Mom was walking from one end of the cabin to the other. She heard her tell Luke Mommy was on the phone. "Here he is," Mom said.

"Hi, buddy," Cynthia said.

"Mommy?" came a groggy reply. Cynthia burst into tears and covered her mouth, hoping Luke wouldn't hear.

"Mommy?" he said again. She started to speak, and the sobs came anyway. "What's wrong, Mommy?"

"They're happy tears, bud. I'm just so happy to hear your voice. I miss you."

"I miss you too, Mommy."

"You have a good sleep. Can you put Grandma back on the phone, please?"

Mom asked again if she should come to the hospital. As much

as Cynthia wanted to see Luke, she knew he was safe. He should be sleeping, and there was no sense disrupting his routine until she knew more about Ben's condition.

"No, please, stay there where I know you're all safe. I'll come out as soon as I can." An escape to the cabin seemed like a good idea about now.

"Be careful, dear."

"Don't worry, Mom."

Cynthia hung up and handed the phone back to Kelly, who'd seemed preoccupied with her fingernails. Warren stepped up from behind her.

"Ready to go to the hospital?"

"Just about." Who was she kidding? The longer she prolonged the hospital visit, the longer she could hope Ben was still alive. She wasn't sure if Warren had called in for an update on Ben's condition, and she didn't want to know. He'd likely have some news once they were alone in the squad car.

Cynthia looked back to where Paul lay dead on the rooftop. She shook her head in disgust as a man from the coroner's office zipped up the body bag.

"Let's go," she said to Warren as she took off the blanket and handed it back to the EMT who'd checked her out.

"Wouldn't hurt to get checked out again at the hospital," he said. Cynthia rolled her eyes. Other than her head pounding and her hearing fading from normal to sounding as if she were under water, she felt as good as she could, given the circumstances.

Cynthia and Warren descended the stairs leading from the rooftop to the hall. As they passed Paul's apartment, she motioned to Warren she was going inside. Two officers Cynthia hadn't met before were processing evidence. They stopped for a moment and looked at Cynthia as if they were going to say something about her crossing the crime scene tape, but she didn't give them a chance.

"There was a coat here earlier," she said to the officer closest to her while gesturing to the chair at the island.

"Did you see a coat?" The first officer looked at the other, eyebrows raised.

"No. There was no coat there when I got here." The other officer continued fingerprinting the table.

"Did you see anyone leaving the apartment wearing a purple coat?" Cynthia asked.

"Can't say I did."

Warren tapped Cynthia's arm with the back of his hand. "What are you thinking?"

"Paul forced me to sit at this table, and I remember seeing a coat there." She gestured to the chair at the island again. "I remember, because I've seen that coat before. It's not a common colour for a raincoat."

"Where did you see it before?"

"Cooper Downs. It was hanging on the back of the door in the CFO's office."

Warren rubbed the five o'clock shadow on his chin. "Officers, see what you can find out about that coat. I'm taking Ms. Webber to the hospital."

"Do you think someone was here when Paul was forcing me to have dinner with him?" The thought gave Cynthia the heebie-jeebies.

"Either that or they came back and got their coat while you were on the roof." Warren put his hand on Cynthia's back and directed her into the hallway. "Come on. Let's get you to the hospital."

41

On the way to the hospital, Warren lectured Cynthia about lying to him and going to Cooper Downs by herself. Then, at Cynthia's request, he told her Ben had died. He'd died by the time the ambulance got to the hospital.

After being checked out by a doctor and getting a couple stitches along her hairline, Cynthia went straight to Linda's room.

"Holy shit! What happened to you?" asked Linda.

"I don't even know where to start." Cynthia walked like a zombie to the edge of Linda's bed and sat. Through tears, she told Linda about Ben.

"I'm such an idiot!" she said, her hand flying to her forehead. "Ow." Besides the stitches, she had two good-sized welts from where Paul had shoved his gun into her cheek and forehead.

"What is it?" asked Linda.

"I should have known Randy was lying to me about the ME's report. It was all in the journal."

"What do you mean? How could a dead woman write about her own death?"

"Maris wrote about getting a tattoo on her foot. An amaryllis flower for her name. It was her first tattoo and she wrote about how worried she was her mom was going to be upset."

"You're not making any sense, Cyn. Are you sure the doctor said you were fine?"

Cynthia started to cry again. "That night at Ben's apartment. He said he thought the body was female because she had a rose tattoo on her foot." She paused to get a Kleenex out of her purse, dab her eyes, and blow her nose. "I remember because he joked about it not being manly, and he thought the body was a woman." She sputtered and dabbed at her eyes again. "I should have known Randy was lying to me from the beginning!"

"It's not your fault," Linda said, extending an arm and wrapping her friend in a hug, which caused Cynthia to sob even more. "It's okay."

"How can you say that?" Cynthia continued sobbing into Linda's shoulder, both of them now lying in Linda's hospital bed. "Ben's dead! It's not okay! This would never have happened if I hadn't gone back to the station!"

"Ben's dead?" came Mom's shocked voice from the doorway. Cynthia jerked her head up.

"Mom! What are you doing here?" She got up and walked to the door. "Where's Luke?"

"He's with your father at our place. I've been trying to call you."

"I'm sorry. I lost my phone."

"Is Ben really dead?" Mom's eyes started to well up. Then they widened at the sight of Cynthia's stitches and the bruises on her face.

Cynthia nodded in response. "It was an accident. He and Randy struggled, and Randy's gun went off. He was trying to protect me."

"Protect you from Randy?" Mom wiped tears from her cheek.

"It's a long story. I'm sorry. I didn't want to tell you any of this over the phone." She put her arms around Mom and Mom squeezed back.

"I hope this story involves telling me what happened to your face."

"Why don't you come in, Gayle?" Linda motioned for Mom to have a seat on her bed.

"I don't get it, Cyn. Why would Randy ask you to help him find Maris if he knew she was dead? That doesn't make any sense." Mom gave Linda a little pat on her shin as she sat on the edge of her bed.

"I don't know. Obviously, he didn't want me to know Maris was dead. I still need to talk to him and sort that out. He'd been about to tell me something when Ben attacked him." Cynthia pulled one of the guest chairs away from the wall and took a seat. She leaned back, crossed her arms, and let out a sigh.

Mom looked at Cynthia, tears still glistening in her eyes. "Why don't you come home with me, try to get some sleep?"

"I don't know how much sleep I'll get tonight. I could use a cup of tea and a hot bath though. And half a dozen pain pills."

Mom smiled. "Anything you need, dear. I'm so sorry this happened to you."

"I wish I could get out of here and come with you," Linda said from the bed.

"I know you do." Cynthia looked at Mom. "Before we go, there's something else you two should know. You're going to find out soon enough anyway." Mom's eyes grew wide again and Linda raised an eyebrow like she always did when she was about to hear a good news story.

"Well, out with it. Don't keep us waiting," said Linda.

Cynthia looked at Mom. "The reason I wasn't answering my phone is because I lost it. I was kidnapped."

Mom gasped and Linda looked like she was about to jump out of her bed.

"Kidnapped?" asked Mom, clutching Linda's arm.

"Was it him? The guy who attacked me?" asked Linda.

"His name's Paul. Or, it was Paul." Cynthia looked at the pristine hospital floor. "I shot him."

Linda gasped. "Oh my god!"

Mom put her hand on her heart, speechless.

"Wait. What?" asked Linda. Cynthia knew Linda had heard her just fine even though her question said otherwise.

"I got a text saying someone had Luke at the Cooper Downs stables. Paul was head of security there. I thought I was being sneaky, peeking into the stable windows, but that's when I got this." She pointed to the stitched-up gash at her hairline.

"Stitch sisters," said Linda with a smirk. "Yours match the ones on the back of my head." Leave it to Linda to try and be funny at a time like this.

"Why didn't you let the police handle it?" Mom had told Cynthia she was fearful something like this would happen with her working for the police.

"They warned me about getting anyone else involved. I know it was stupid. I wasn't thinking. I just wanted Luke back."

"Well, it's over now. Let your mom take you home," Linda said as she touched Mom's hand. "Have a glass of wine. Try to forget about everything. I know better than to tell you to try and get some sleep."

"I think I'm going to need something a lot stronger than wine."

"We have that too," Mom piped up.

"I'd really like to see my little man even if it's just to watch him sleep." Cynthia stood and put the chair back against the wall. Mom gave Linda another pat on the shin then grabbed Cynthia's hand.

"How did you know I'd be here still?" Cynthia asked.

"When you weren't home, I figured you'd be with your best friend." Mom glanced at Linda on her way out and gave her a thankful smile.

42

The next morning, Cynthia woke to the sound of Luke's voice.

"Mommy," he whispered, touching her cheek with his pint-sized fingers. As predicted, she hadn't slept much. After a couple drinks with Mom, she'd stared at the TV before realizing nothing she was seeing was registering, so she'd climbed into bed with Luke and dozed off for a couple hours.

"Morning, buddy." She took his hand and gave it a little squeeze. "How'd you sleep?"

"Good." He sat up and looked around the room, a puzzled look on his face.

"We're at Grandma and Grandpa's," she said.

"I know, Mommy. Can we read a story?"

"Of course, but I need to tell you something first." She sat up and faced her son. Might as well get this over with. She closed her eyes, took a breath, and placed an arm around Luke.

"Something really bad happened last night." Luke's eyes got big, and he sat as still as was possible for a four-year-old first thing in the morning. Cynthia took a deep, shaky breath. "Ben died."

"He died? Like Daddy?"

"Yes, sweetie."

"No! I don't want Ben to die," he cried.

"Neither do I." She fought back tears and lifted Luke onto her lap so she could squeeze him tight. She rocked him for a minute or two while they both cried. Cynthia's tears fell silently, and Luke wailed. Eventually his wails subdued to gentle sobs then he stopped and looked up at Cynthia.

"Is Ben with Daddy now?"

Cynthia swallowed hard, trying to rid herself of the scorching lump in her throat. "Yeah, baby, he's with Daddy."

"I'm glad Daddy has a friend now." Cynthia broke down into full-on sobs and squeezed Luke tighter in her arms. She managed to squeeze out a "Me too" before Luke said, "Mommy, you're squishing me." Cynthia released him instantly.

"Sorry, buddy." She wiped away the tears and pulled a Kleenex from the box on the nightstand. "You want to read that book now?"

"Yeah," Luke said, hopping off the bed and running to the shelf where Mom kept a small stash of picture books for when Luke visited. She hoped a story would calm them both down.

***

Despite everything that had happened, Cynthia was eager to get to work and grill Randy about what he had been going to tell her.

She thought about checking her phone for messages then remembered she didn't have it. Warren would give her an update when she gave him her statements. She'd do that first thing. No sense putting it off. Reliving last night's terrible nightmare was the last thing she wanted to do. Two shootings in one night—one where she'd pulled the trigger herself. How had all this happened?

"Morning, Cyn." Mom's chipper voice pulled Cynthia from her thoughts.

"Morning." She glanced at the clock on the stove. It was just after 6:30 a.m. "What are you doing up so early?"

"I was worried about you. You've lost two men you've cared about in close to that many years."

"I'm all right, Mom. I just need to focus on Luke right now." She gave Mom a hug then looked in the fridge for something to eat.

"Who's Kelinda?" Mom asked.

"Kelinda?" Cynthia remembered Hack's story about Kelinda White being the only programmer in his school with skills as good as his.

"Yeah. Her name showed up on my phone when you called last night."

"Of course." Cynthia threw her arms up in the air. "Mom, Kelly is Kelinda." She placed her hands on Mom's shoulders and gave them a shake.

"Who's Kelly?"

"Kelly White. She's Kelinda!" Cynthia paced excitedly in the kitchen. "She's the one responsible for the fake winning tickets. It has to be her." She tucked her hair behind her ear. "I need to get to the office," she said, grabbing several granola bars.

"Um, dear, I—"

"Dammit! My car's at Cooper Downs. Can you drop me off?"

"Of course. I'll just tell your father he's in charge."

"Luke will like that. Tell Dad no cake for breakfast. I'm going to tell Luke what I'm doing."

"But, it's Saturday," Mom called after her.

"Criminals don't care, Mom, and neither does law enforcement."

"Right. Silly me."

***

Cynthia ducked into the bathroom to splash some cool water on her face after chatting with Luke. Without fresh clothes or makeup, that would have to be enough to get her through the morning, then she'd run home at lunch and change.

Mom appeared at the bathroom door.

"You sure you have to do this now?"

"I'm sure. I need to finish giving Warren my statements anyway. They're probably holding Randy until I confirm Ben's shooting was an accident. I was the only one that saw Ben attack him."

"All right. I gave your father strict orders for Luke's breakfast." The way Mom tapped her pointer finger in the air made Cynthia smile.

"Are you in trouble, Mommy?" Luke said from behind Mom.

"No, but Grandpa's gonna be if he doesn't take good care of you." She stepped into the hallway and knelt so she was level with Luke. "I'll be back as soon as I can, okay?"

"Okay, Mommy." Luke gave Cynthia a hug.

"Love you, bud."

43

The closer she got to the station, the angrier Cynthia felt. She couldn't bear to throw out the wilted roses in the backseat even though their scent made her sick. Why did Ben have to attack Randy? If he'd only stayed in the car. And Randy, how could he keep the ME's report from her? Why did he have to pull his gun?

Clearly there was more going on than she knew, and she was going to get to the bottom of it. Knowing Randy would be held until she finished telling Warren what happened last night, she went upstairs to see Hack first. She took the stairs two at a time and marched straight to Hack's desk.

"Hi, doll." Hack stood, his face deadpan. There was an awkward pause. "Sorry to hear about your beau."

Right. Cynthia remembered how things were when Jason had died. People became weird around her, not sure if she was going to cry if they mentioned him. She suspected things would be similar this time around. Most people weren't comfortable with other people's tears.

"Thanks." She smiled but had no time to make other people feel better. "There's a woman who works at the Cooper Downs stables. Goes by Kelly White. I think it's Kelinda. Do you remember what she looks like?" She was talking so fast, Hack didn't have a chance to interrupt. "If I found a picture, could you confirm Kelly and Kelinda are the same person?"

"For sure, doll. One never forgets a fellow hacker. Especially one that good. I'm quite certain it's her though."

"What makes you so sure?"

"I found a signature in the code used to get into Cooper Downs's network. I wasn't sure at first. Kelly wasn't much of a bragger, so I wouldn't have expected her to leave a signature. But some asshole threatened her when we were in school. Made her hack into his student record and change his grade. Told her if she didn't leave a signature, he wouldn't pay her for to change his grade. It's the same code I found on the Cooper Downs network. I think she wanted to get caught."

"What did he threaten her with?"

"Said he was going to beat up her little brother. Their parents had died a few months earlier. He was the only family she had."

"Do you remember the asshole's name?"

"Oh yeah. We were all scared shitless of that bully. Paul Lennings."

"Jesus! That's the fucker who kidnapped me."

"Shit, doll. You know, everyone was talking about you this morning. We weren't sure if you were going to make it in today. We were told to keep an eye on you. Make sure you're okay."

"Wait a minute. It's Saturday. What are *you* doing here?"

Hack shrugged. "I don't sleep much, and criminals don't take a break on the weekends, so why should we?" Hack asked.

Cynthia nodded, a small smirk on her face as she remembered what she'd told Mom earlier. "I thought maybe being in cybercrimes, you had a different schedule."

"Nope."

"So, Paul, he was studying programming?"

"Yeah, probably had aspirations of bullying people online too."

"Was he ever reported?"

"No. We all knew he'd threatened Kelinda, but we didn't want her to get in trouble for changing his grade. She disappeared after that year was over. The next year, with nobody to bully, Paul failed and dropped out."

"He didn't try to threaten someone else?"

"Oh, he did. None of us had anything he could hold over us like Kelinda did."

"Shit. He must have tracked her down and thought he could make some big bucks at the track without anyone finding out."

"Doesn't really sound like something Kelinda would be into, but Paul knows her weak spot," said Hack.

"I need to talk to her. Any chance you know her address?"

"We're the police. We know everyone's address. And I already sent it to you."

"Really?"

"When I found the signature in the code, I looked up Kelinda. Her address is in an email I sent you last night."

"Perfect, thanks." Cynthia hurried off as quickly as she'd arrived.

"Wait. There's something you should know, doll." Hack called after her, but Cynthia was already on her way to Warren's office.

44

Cynthia and Warren sat in Warren's office with the door closed. Although his office was smaller than Randy's, it was so tidy that it seemed a lot bigger.

"You ready?" Warren asked, a recorder on his desk.

"As ready as I'm gonna be," she replied.

She took a quick breath in through her nose and exhaled loudly through her mouth, her shoulders visibly sagging. Warren pressed record, and Cynthia closed her eyes and proceeded to recount the events that transpired down the hall less than twenty-four hours ago. When she was finished reliving the nightmare of Ben's death, Warren paused the recorder.

"You need a break?"

"I'm fine."

"I need to ask you some more questions about Paul and the kidnapping."

"Of course." Cynthia nodded. "I have some new information about Paul, thanks to Hack, so I'd like to get this over with. I've got a witness to question."

Warren raised his eyebrows and started the recorder again. When they were finished, Warren escorted Cynthia to Randy's cell. He stood as soon as he saw them coming.

"I'll leave you two to talk," Warren said.

"Thank you," Cynthia said turning to Randy. She saw his mouth open.

"Just let me get this out," Cynthia said, cutting him off before he had a chance to form any words. Randy stared at her through the cell bars and waited for her to speak. His eyes were solemn.

"Warren will be letting you out as soon as we're done. I know what happened was an accident." Cynthia felt her face flush and tears fill her eyes. She looked away from Randy to regain her composure. "I don't know how the gun went off. I don't understand why you were pointing it at me in the first place, but I know in my heart you're not a killer."

She held up her hand, indicating she wasn't done. She took a breath and continued. "But why lie to me about Maris? Why ask me to look for her when you knew she was already dead?" Cynthia paused, and waited for Randy to respond.

"I . . . I want you to know how truly sorry I am." Randy's eyes and cheeks turned red, and Cynthia could see tears forming in his eyes. "What I said last night was the truth. I fucked up. I let desperation get the better of me." He covered his eyes with his hand for a moment. "Oh, God." He cried, keeping his hand over his eyes, only removing them to find a seat on the cot in the cell.

"What do you mean desperation?" Thinking this might take a while, Cynthia took Randy's lead and sat in one of the visitor chairs.

"A few months ago, I was on my way home from a brutal domestic murder. After this long working homicides, the brutality of it all doesn't usually register with me, but I knew the couple. The three of us had gone to high school together."

Cynthia remained silent. She felt for him. That had to have been one of the most difficult scenes he'd ever worked, but she couldn't help wondering what this had to do with Maris's case.

"I was driving near the casino and decided to stop in for a drink to clear my head. The drinking led to trying my hand at a few card games. It happened several nights in a row. I lost thousands of dollars in one week and became obsessed with winning my money back. I kept thinking the next time I played, I'd win big. It never happened." Randy hung his head.

Cynthia remembered how terrible Randy had looked and smelled the other day. He looked as if he'd been up all night. Was he still gambling?

"Then Kat came back to help put your old boss away, and I

wanted to change. Something about seeing her again made me realize I was on a rocky path. But it was too late. I'd already racked up so much debt just trying to break even." Randy rubbed his hand across both eyebrows then up through his greasy hair.

Cynthia wanted to tell Randy everything would be okay, but she wasn't sure she believed it.

"I'm sure now Vivian had been watching me the whole time, just waiting for me to be at most my desperate. She told me she could help." Randy paused and Cynthia jumped in, not able to hold her silence any longer.

"What did she do?" she asked.

"She offered to pay all my debts if I did one thing for her."

Cynthia straightened in her chair, remembering Vivian and Paul together that night at Ben's. "She wanted you to look the other way."

Randy nodded, looked up at the ceiling then back at Cynthia. "Then she broke into my house and drugged my dog."

"What?" Although Cynthia had yet to meet Vivian, she was starting to get a pretty clear picture of who she was.

"Nobody messes with my dog. So, I started formulating a plan. I know I'll face consequences for what I've done, but I've been tracking Vivian's every move. I think I know how to bring her down."

"I'm not sure, but I think she was at Paul's when he kidnapped me. I saw her coat, but it was gone by the time Warren and the guys got there."

"It wouldn't surprise me if she had been there. Paul's not bright enough to have engineered this himself. That guy's an arrogant meathead."

"Was," Cynthia corrected. "I think you're right. Formulating a detailed plan to claim unpaid winnings seems beyond him." Cynthia tugged on a stray piece of hair then tucked it behind her ear. "At first, I thought maybe he'd heard a news story about unclaimed winning tickets and had tried to run with it. I hear those copycat crime stories all the time," said Cynthia.

"After following Vivian's every move and watching the two of them interact, my money's on Vivian calling the shots," Randy added, then paused. "Sorry, bad choice of words," he said.

"I need to follow up on a lead from Hack. I think Paul was threatening one of his coworkers to do his dirty work for him. Or maybe it was Vivian's dirty work?"

Warren cleared his throat behind Cynthia. She moved out of the way so he could get to Randy and watched him unlock the cell.

"You're free to go for now, Detective," Warren said. "You know the drill. Don't leave the area. Your badge and weapon will remain here until everything is cleared up."

"Of course." Randy stepped out of the cell.

"Wanda's got your belongings at the front," Warren said to Randy.

As Cynthia started to head in the direction of her office, Warren turned to her and said, "We recovered your cellphone from Cooper Downs. Wanda's got that too."

"Perfect. Thanks, Warren." Cynthia gave a little wave in Warren's direction and took a sharp right to reception rather than going straight down the hall to her office. Randy followed a few feet behind.

Cynthia's cellphone was waiting for her on the reception counter. "Thanks, Wanda."

"You got it," replied Wanda.

Randy wasn't quick enough to get out of Cynthia's way as she turned to head to her office, and the two ended up face-to-face.

"You know . . . I really am sorry," he said, quietly.

"I know." Cynthia put her head down and stepped around Randy. Then she lifted her head so her eyes met his. "But it doesn't change the fact my boyfriend is in the morgue." She continued to her office.

45

Cynthia fired up her laptop and searched for the email from Hack containing Kelly's address. She was hoping it was early enough she could catch Kelly at home. Though Cynthia flagged the email in case she forgot the address while on the road, she was sure she'd remember. She had a photographic memory when it came to numbers and still remembered phone numbers from people she'd long since lost touch with.

Kelly and her brother didn't live far from the station, which gave Cynthia hope she could make it there before having to fight the morning rush hour. After fifteen minutes or so on the road, Cynthia arrived in Renfrew, the northeast Calgary neighbourhood where Kelly and her brother, Christian, lived.

She found their house right away. A small character home on 9th Avenue with stairs and a ramp leading up to the front porch. Cynthia chose the stairs. It was light blue with white trim in need of a fresh coat of paint. She rang the doorbell, and moments later, a blonde woman about her age opened the door, a puzzled expression on her face.

"Hi," Cynthia said. "Is Kelly home? I wanted to thank her for her help last night." She felt bad being untruthful about the real reason she was there but didn't see the need to alarm the blonde.

"Oh, heavens! Are you the one who was kidnapped last night?"

Cynthia smiled, surprised the blonde knew so much.

"Yes, I'm Cynthia." She left it at that. No need to mention the police just yet. She extended her right hand.

"I'm Mel." Mel accepted the hand Cynthia offered and gave it a gentle shake. Cynthia heard a high-pitched whirring as a teenager in an electric wheelchair pulled up next to Mel. "This is

Christian, Kelinda's brother."

"It's nice to meet you, Christian." Cynthia held out her hand to Christian, and he shakily reached for it with a hand that curved severely at his wrist.

"Hi," he said. Mel used the hand towel on Christian's lap to wipe his mouth.

"I'm sorry." She looked at Cynthia. "We're just finishing breakfast." Turning back to Christian, she said, "It's okay, Christian. Cynthia and I are going to talk for a moment. Why don't you go finish your breakfast, and then we can go to school?"

Christian used the joystick on his wheelchair to turn around and head back to the table visible from the front door.

"Christian's graduating from high school this year," Mel said, a proud look on her face. She lowered her voice a bit then said, "I'm Christian's caregiver when Kelinda's working." Things were becoming clearer for Cynthia.

"Has she already gone to work then?"

"Yes. The poor thing's up at the crack of dawn to get out to that racetrack. Spends much of her free time working too, after Christian's gone to bed. Can I give her a message for you?"

"That's all right. I'll take a drive by Cooper Downs and see if I can catch her there. Do you live here too?"

"I do have a room here, but I don't live here. Sometimes when Kelinda needs me late, it's just easier to crash here. I've been working with Christian since he started school."

"That's wonderful," Cynthia said.

"Kelinda is a very talented computer programmer." Mel beamed with pride again. "She takes on programming jobs on the side."

"That's impressive." If she'd doubted this was the same Kelinda Hack knew, she certainly had no doubt now.

"Okay. Well, I'll mention you stopped by in case you miss her."

"Thank you. I appreciate it." Cynthia peered a little further into the house. The inside seemed in much better shape than the outside, fully updated with modern decor. "Nice to meet you, Christian." Christian looked up from his breakfast and gave Cynthia a wave. "Congratulations on your graduation," she said, and Christian grinned a big toothy smile at her.

"He doesn't say much," Mel said. "You were lucky to get a 'hi' earlier. He mostly uses his tablet to communicate." She smiled.

"Thanks, again," Cynthia said and took the steps back to her car. She looked up as she put the car in gear. Mel stood with the door open, and the two women waved in unison as Cynthia drove away.

***

Randy arrived home thankful he had the kind of relationship with his neighbours that allowed him to phone them at a moment's notice and request a favour—check on Boo. He'd done it numerous times in the past, and because the retired Dennisons knew he was a cop, they were happy to help him out whenever he needed them. This time though, he hadn't explained he was detained in a cell rather than his office.

"Thank you for watching Boo."

"It's our pleasure, Randy. He's such a good boy."

"I may need to go away for a while. Would you mind if Boo stayed with you?"

"Of course not. Whatever you need."

Boo jumped up and down in the Dennison's back yard. His tongue flopped around as he ran to get his ball. All Randy wanted to do was take a shower and wash away the sweat and bad luck from the past twenty-four hours. He opened the gate in the fence separating his yard from the Dennison's and threw Boo's ball from the Dennison's yard to his.

"Thanks again," he said. He left Boo in the yard while he walked to his bedroom to check on the stash of cash Kat had helped him obtain. It was gone. He hoped that meant Vivian was gone too. He texted Warren.

She took the bait.

46

Thankfully, Cooper Downs wasn't far from Renfrew. The morning rush hour was just getting started. Cynthia was headed in the opposite direction of most of the commuters though, so she hadn't noticed the surge of traffic yet. She parked at the back of the stables and could see Kelly exercising one of the thoroughbreds in a small warm-up ring near the stables. Then she stopped the horse and stroked its nose. Cynthia could tell from the movement of her lips she was talking to the steed.

Cynthia sat for a moment. It couldn't have been easy for Kelly losing her parents, let alone raising her brother. Cynthia guessed Christian had cerebral palsy. He would need constant care for the rest of his life. She thought about that bastard Paul and what he'd done to Maris. If he knew about Christian, it wouldn't take much to get Kelly to do whatever he asked.

She got out of the car, and Kelly looked in her direction at the sound of the car door thudding shut. Aside from last night's tragic events and the reason for Cynthia's visit to Cooper Downs, it was a beautiful morning. Cynthia could see the Rocky Mountains ever so faintly across the horizon. The sun glistened off the lush green grass bordering the parking lot. Kelly looked at Cynthia.

"Cynthia?"

"Morning, Kelly." Cynthia walked towards Kelly. As she got closer, she could see a bruise near Kelly's chin.

"I thought you'd be at home resting after the ordeal Paul put you through last night. I hate that I had a part in all that," said Kelly.

"It's okay," Cynthia said. "What happened to your chin?"

Kelly reached for her jaw as if she'd forgotten about it.

"Paul knocked me out after he used my phone to text you about your son." She swallowed and looked away.

"I just came from your house," Cynthia continued.

Kelly's eyes grew big and her face turned white. "My house?"

"I'd hoped to catch you before your workday started." Cynthia glanced at the chestnut horse patiently standing by. "I met your brother."

"Oh." Kelly seemed confused.

"You and I have a mutual acquaintance."

"Oh?" Repeating herself, but this time questioning Cynthia.

"Hack . . . uh, I mean Harvey Ack—"

"He's always been Hack to me." Kelly laughed. "I'd heard he was working for the police now."

"Then you know why I'm here?"

"I'm afraid I do." Kelly stroked the horse's nose, who reciprocated by nodding his head. "This is Chipper's Pride III." She laughed at the way the name sounded and looked at the ground. "I call him Chip."

"He seems to like you."

"I'm better with animals, you know. People aren't really my thing."

"Sounds like most computer programmers," Cynthia said, directing the conversation back to the topic at hand. She cringed at the blatant stereotype.

"I'm sure Hack told you about what happened with Paul in university." Kelly looked into Cynthia's eyes and Cynthia nodded. "My parents were ranchers before they died," Kelly continued. "The ranch was too much for Christian and I to keep up. We sold it and moved into the city, so we could both be close to school. After what happened with Paul, I hadn't wanted anyone to exploit my talent or threaten my brother like that again, so I left school."

"He threatened you, Kelly. Why didn't you tell someone?"

"It was hard enough being the only woman in computer engineering that year. And I was good on top of that. I hated the attention I was already getting for excelling. I just wanted to be left alone, but I especially wanted to make sure Christian was okay." She gestured for Cynthia to follow her and Chip into the stables. "I thought I could come here and disappear from all that."

"Did Paul follow you here?"

"I'm not sure. I don't think so. I'd hoped it was just a coincidence."

"How long have you worked here?"

"Almost five years." Kelly led Chip into his stall, took off his halter, then closed the gate, securing him inside. He exhaled loudly through his nose, expressing his disapproval at being back in his stall.

"Was Vivian here when you started?"

"Yes." The two women walked back to where they'd entered the stables, and Kelly hung the tack with the other leads and halters on the wall. She took off her work gloves and set them on a shelf while Cynthia contemplated her next question. The yellow logo on a pair of gloves on the bottom shelf caught Cynthia's eye. Cynthia pointed to them.

"Do you mind if I take these?" Cynthia asked, remembering Paul hadn't been wearing gloves last night.

"Go ahead," Kelly said. "I never use those ones. They were missing for a while."

Cynthia picked up the gloves. As she inspected them, she became even more sure they were the gloves Paul was wearing when he killed Maris and attacked Linda. She carefully tucked them in her bag.

Cynthia and Kelly stepped out of the stables. Kelly looked around as if checking for other staff members before continuing.

"I've yet to meet Vivian," Cynthia continued. "She always seems to be in meetings, and she doesn't return my calls."

"Convenient." Kelly raised her eyebrows. "I don't see her much other than sometimes when I drop my timesheet off at the admin office."

"Do you think Paul was smart enough to come up with this ticket scam on his own? He'd have to know where to look in the accounting records to find the unclaimed ticket numbers."

"I didn't ask questions. Just did what he told me to."

"What did he have on you?"

"You mean besides threatening Christian?"

"Yes. Though I suppose that's enough in itself."

"It was that stupid stunt from university." Kelly broke eye contact with Cynthia and continued. "My parents had died a few months before that, and I wasn't sure what was going to happen with their estate. They'd never really talked about that kind of stuff, and I wasn't sure if I'd have enough money to look after Christian, so when Paul said he'd pay me to change his grades, I agreed." She kicked the dirt and made eye contact again. "It was really stupid. It wasn't even that much money."

"Did he pay you to hack into the Cooper Downs network?"

"No, I just did it because I wanted him to leave me and Christian alone. I like it here. I didn't want to get fired. He told me he'd have me fired if I didn't do what he said. I believed he could."

"Did you ever see Vivian and Paul together? Maybe hear what they were up to?"

Kelly shook her head. "I wish I could be more helpful. Paul brought me ticket numbers and I recreated them. That's about it."

"You've been great. I'll need you to stop by the police station and complete an official statement as soon as possible."

"I'll stop by later today."

"Thanks, Kelly." Cynthia stood and shook Kelly's hand. "Don't worry. I'll get to the bottom of this," said Cynthia.

"I deserve whatever's coming my way. I just hope Christian will be okay," said Kelly.

"You were just doing what you had to," said Cynthia. She turned to walk back to her car when Kelly called after her.

"Hey, how's your reporter friend doing?"

Cynthia paused and turned around to look at Kelly. She'd seen the woman twice, and both times she'd asked about Linda. "She's still in the hospital, but she's going to be just fine."

"Glad to hear it. I miss seeing her on the news."

"So do I, Kelly. So do I."

The Cooper Downs administration office stood out against the backdrop of the Rocky Mountains like it was beckoning to her. Another look through Vivian's office couldn't hurt.

"Thanks for your help. I'll let Wanda, our receptionist, know you'll be stopping by later." Kelly waved as she disappeared into the stables.

47

After arguing with herself about whether to walk or drive to the casino, Cynthia drove to the front parking lot near the Cooper Downs main entrance rather than walk across the grass and racetrack that separated the casino from the stables. As she parked her car, she glanced at the clock on her dash. It was almost 9 a.m., the time Ben would normally have called to say good morning. She shook her head. She couldn't let herself think about him right now. Not while Vivian was still out there.

She arrived at the admin office, and the receptionist was nowhere to be found. Of course—it was Saturday. Cynthia was looking at the locked door trying to come up with another plan when Sherie came around the corner, keys in hand.

"Cynthia!" She sounded chipper and flashed Cynthia a friendly smile. "Have you come to have another look through Maris's desk?"

"Actually, I was hoping to have another look through Vivian's office." Cynthia doubted Sherie knew about last night's events.

Sherie nodded as she unlocked the main door to the admin offices and turned on the lights. "That's odd," she said, looking towards Vivian's office.

"What?" Cynthia followed closely behind.

"Vivian usually leaves her door closed at night." Sherie glanced into Vivian's dark office. "And it looks like her laptop is gone." She turned to face Cynthia and rolled her eyes. "I guess she's eluded you again." Her voice had a frustrated tone to it. "And it looks like I'll be on my own with the bookkeeping today." She let out a huff. "I guess that's to be expected on a Saturday, but Vivian hasn't been here much all week. I thought she might put in some extra hours today too."

"Sherie, there's something I need to tell you. Can we sit down?" Cynthia meandered to Sherie's desk.

"Sounds serious, dear," she said, pulling out her chair.

"I'm afraid it is." Cynthia summarized the events involving Maris as best she could. She left Maris's death until the end. "I'm so sorry, Sherie. I know you two were close."

"This is Vivian's fault, isn't it?" Sherie grabbed a Kleenex from the box on her desk and dabbed her eyes.

"Well, we're still trying to piece it all together." Cynthia remembered how many times Maris had written about Vivian in her journal and how her last entry had been about Vivian wanting her to come for dinner so they could talk about Maris going back to work.

Sherie sniffled then said, "Maris told me a lot of things about Vivian. Would it help if I wrote them down?"

"Without Maris here to confirm them, it's all just hearsay, so I'm not sure it would."

"What if I'd heard something I wasn't supposed to?" Sherie stared coldly into Cynthia's eyes.

"Did you?"

"I might have." Sherie's cheeks flushed and her eyes squinted as if she was trying to remember something.

"It's still your word against Vivian's, but with Maris's journal to back it up, it might help."

"I'm sure I can come up with something," Sherie said, squinting her eyes again. Cynthia wasn't sure she liked the sound of that. She knew Sherie thought of Maris more like a daughter than a coworker and would likely do anything to help her. It seemed more and more like Sherie viewed Vivian as an evil boss.

"I'm guessing it might be a while before Vivian is back to work now that her son is dead," Cynthia said. She hadn't told Sherie the part about being the one responsible for Paul's death, although she wasn't sure Sherie would care.

"Oh, I'm used to holding down the fort around here. I'll call head office and see if they can send someone out to help for a while. Vivian was supposed to have done that months ago," said Sherie. Cynthia was surprised at how quickly Sherie recovered from the news of Maris's death. She guessed she was probably so busy that continuing as if nothing was wrong was her only option.

Cynthia touched Sherie's arm as she stood to go have another look through Vivian's office. "I'm sorry about Maris," she said and smiled a sad, lopsided smile.

As she stood in Vivian's office, a rush of cold came over Cynthia. She turned on the lights. The walls were bare except for the brighter squares where paintings and photos once hung, protecting the walls' surfaces from sun damage.

"Uh . . . Sherie? It looks like Vivian might be gone a long time."

Sherie jumped up from her desk to see what Cynthia was talking about. "Shit," she said, instantly covering her mouth. Her cheeks went red. "Head office will want to hear about this too." She spun on her heels and went back to work on the payroll.

Cynthia went behind the executive style mahogany desk and sat in Vivian's chair. The desk was completely clean, almost sterile. Cynthia was sure there had been picture frames and knick-knacks on its surface yesterday.

Digging in her bag, she pulled out her phone and texted Hack, asking him for Vivian's address. Cynthia was going to talk to her face-to-face if it was the last thing she did today. To Cynthia's surprise, Hack texted back right away. She read the address and burst into tears. It was the penthouse at Ben's apartment building.

48

Back at police headquarters, Randy was pacing back and forth in Warren's office. All he wanted to do was make everything right.

"How exactly do you see this playing out?" asked Warren, trying his best to keep an open mind while Randy explained his plan for Vivian. Sitting on the corner of his desk, Warren watched this man he still thought of as his boss even though he'd been suspended pending further investigation.

"Look, Warren, I know I need to earn your trust back. I would have already handed in my resignation if it weren't for Vivian. I can't let her get away with this. I know she's the one pulling the strings."

"Do you have any evidence against her?"

"Other than her bribing me to protect her son, breaking into my house, and drugging my dog?" Randy was waving his arms around like a lunatic. "I think that's plenty, don't you?" He put his hands on his hips and finally made eye contact with Warren, waiting for his response.

"I'm sure Vivian could spin all that any way she likes. We need something linking her to Maris's murder."

"She's too smart for that, but sooner or later, she's going to screw up. Greed will get the better of her."

"It's not like we can put a guy on her 24/7."

"Why not? All I want to do is catch this bitch. Yeah, I was wrong to take her bribe. The minute I agreed, I regretted it. I was desperate, and now I'm going to pay the price. Let putting her away be the last thing I do before I resign."

"Jesus. You know this isn't my call."

"Then talk to the Chief. He owes me one."

"Okay, man. Do what you gotta do. I'll talk to the Chief, but in the meantime, do not make me regret this."

"You won't. An innocent man is dead because of me. That's not the way I wanted this to go down. That's on Vivian, and all I want to do right now is get that bitch." Randy stopped pacing to take a breath. "I mean it. You won't regret this." He thought about the counterfeit money and the tracker he'd gotten from Kat. Warren wouldn't like that either.

Warren took a seat behind his desk. "Get outta here." He gestured at his office door, and Randy took a couple steps in the direction of the hall. "And try to stay out of trouble," said Warren.

"Funny. You, telling *me* to stay out of trouble. I remember not so long ago when things were the other way around." Randy shook his head and looked at his feet as he exhaled, finally calming himself. He shoved his hands in his pockets and looked back at Warren. "I really am sorry to put you in this position."

***

Cynthia hadn't stopped crying since receiving Vivian's address from Hack. It was like every emotion she'd ever felt had come to the surface, refusing to be shoved back down. She'd managed to choke out a few words to Sherie as she'd left Cooper Downs, and Sherie had promised to have her statement to Cynthia by the end of the day.

Driving to Ben's apartment had been difficult with streams of tears blurring her vision. Thankfully, having a four-year-old had trained her to keep lots of Kleenex around. In the twenty minutes it had taken her to get downtown from the casino, she'd gone through the remains of a travel pack she'd found in the glovebox. Rather than searching her bag for more Kleenex while she drove, she'd resorted to wiping her nose with a used Kleenex and dabbing her eyes with her sleeve.

She was parked on the street across from the entrance to the parkade adjoining the building where Ben lived. She thought about the first time she'd given Ben a ride home months ago. It had been the first time she'd thought of him as more than just a coworker. He'd been so sweet to Luke that night. She remembered how he'd wink at her when he smiled, even before they were dating. She looked expectantly at his building, wishing she could see him strut out the entrance one more time. A wail escaped and she rested her head on the arm she had stretched across the steering wheel. She cried until her eyes felt like they were swollen shut.

When she lifted her head, the street was a blur. She took a few uneasy breaths, trying to pull herself together when someone caught her eye. She noticed the purple coat first. It was the same coat she'd seen last night at Vivian's, the same one that had hung on the back of Vivian's office door. The coat was filled out by a woman wearing dark sunglasses and spiked heels. The way she walked reminded Cynthia of a supermodel. It had to be Vivian.

She was walking on Cynthia's side of the street, heading in her direction. Although she couldn't see where the woman was looking with the dark shades, Cynthia slumped down in her seat, hoping Vivian wouldn't look in her car. She didn't look much different than any other woman you might find on the streets of Calgary, flaunting their good fashion sense, but Cynthia sensed she was dangerous.

Suddenly, she snapped into high alert. She blinked her eyes slow and hard, trying to force the blur of tears away. By the time she found her phone, her eyes were focusing. She found Warren's name in her contacts and pressed the green "Call" button. She let her Bluetooth take over while she started her car. Traffic wasn't going to allow her to make a U-turn and follow Vivian. She was going to have to figure out some way to backtrack and try and cut Vivian off.

"Cynthia?" Either Warren was psychic, or he had her in his contacts list.

"Warren. I just saw Vivian. She's on 6th Avenue SW." Cynthia glanced in the rearview. "I think she took a right down 8th Street."

"All right. I'm on it."

"I'll see if I can drive around and cut her off."

"We've got a trace on her. As long as she has her cell, we can find her."

Hearing this relieved Cynthia. She wasn't sure what she'd do if she did catch up to Vivian.

"Why don't you call it a day? You've been through a lot in the last twenty-four hours."

That's for sure. "Soon. I've got some paperwork I need to do first." She wanted to prepare her report while her interviews with Kelly and Sherie were still fresh in her mind.

"Okay. Well, thanks for the tip. Maybe by the time you get back here, we'll have Vivian in custody."

"One can hope." As much as she did hope that was the case, she had a feeling Vivian was smarter than that.

49

After stopping at Mom and Dad's to have lunch and see Luke, Cynthia headed back to the office. Of course, Luke was doing fine. It seemed like knowing Ben was with Jason was all Luke needed for now. There would be questions and times when he'd feel sad about Ben, just as he still did with Jason, and Cynthia would deal with them as they came up.

The office felt oddly quiet when Cynthia returned. She hadn't worked many Saturdays in the few months she'd been with the police, so she didn't have a lot to compare to. It was as if everyone had decided to take their lunch break at the same time. Cynthia dragged herself out of her vehicle. She'd rather be at home napping with Luke. Mom had suggested it, but as much as she needed it, she'd told Kelly and Sherie she'd be waiting for their written statements.

As she passed through the sliding glass doors of the main entrance, Cynthia's phone went off. She reached into her bag, saw it was Linda, and made a mental note to stop by the hospital on her way home. She guessed it was Linda's turn to check up on *her*.

"Cynthia," Wanda said, as she approached reception. "I thought you would have taken the rest of the day off."

"You're not the only one." Cynthia smiled and headed to the row of in-baskets on the counter behind Wanda's desk. There were so many staff members she still had to search for her name. She found it and grabbed the folded sheet of lined paper resting in her mailbox.

Wanda spun around in her chair to face Cynthia. "Oh, Hack's been looking for you. Something about a video you asked him to look at."

"Thanks. I'll check in with him before I leave." She was about to head to her office when she heard her name coming from the entrance. It was Sherie. She was red-faced and out of breath.

"Cynthia," she said again and leaned on the reception counter to catch her breath. "I don't have long before I need to be back at work, but can we talk quickly?"

"Sure. Let's go to my office."

***

Knowing Sherie didn't have time for coffee or water, Cynthia closed her office door and offered Sherie a chair. Before she sat, Sherie eyed Cynthia with a worried mother's look.

"Are you all right? You were so upset when you left."

Cynthia's face flushed at the memory of her outburst and how unprofessional she'd been. "I'll be okay. A lot has happened in the last day."

"I know," Sherie said, reaching out to touch Cynthia's arm. She paused as if she wanted to hug her but wasn't sure she should. After an awkward moment she sat, and Cynthia followed her lead.

"Thank you for your concern," Cynthia said, trying to regain some of her professionalism.

"I think I can help." Sherie pulled an envelope out of her purse. "I . . .uh . . . think this might be what you need." She hesitated then handed Cynthia the envelope.

"Did you remember something Vivian said?"

Sherie looked away and swallowed before returning her gaze to Cynthia. "I think this speaks to Vivian's character." She stood abruptly, avoiding the question. "I should get back to work."

Before Cynthia had a chance to thank her, Sherie was already halfway down the hall. Cynthia paused, not sure if she should chase after her. She wished Sherie had given her a minute to read what was in the envelope, so she could confirm details and ask questions. Cynthia sat at her desk and opened the envelope. There was a yellow sticky note tacked to the front that read,

"I hope this is what you need." Sherie had signed her first name followed by two exclamation marks she'd turned into a smiley face. Cynthia removed the sticky note and read what Sherie had written. The letter confirmed what Maris had written in her journal. Vivian had threatened her employees and broken labour code standards, though this wasn't enough to prove it was her idea to steal from Cooper Downs.

But what Cynthia read on the second page seemed more promising if it was true. Sherie described how Vivian had approached her about making some extra cash and wondered if she knew how to reprint a ticket for a race that had already happened. Vivian was too smart to ask questions like that. She would have known there were controls in place to prevent Sherie from doing that.

Sherie also detailed an argument she'd overheard between Vivian and Paul about which tickets to fake. Why hadn't Sherie mentioned this before? Cynthia would need to confirm these statements before including them in her report. Her sleepless night was starting to affect her. All she wanted to do now was go home. She set Sherie's note aside and saw the piece of paper she'd picked up from her mailbox.

As she unfolded the note, the printing seemed vaguely familiar. All the letters were printed in upper case. She'd seen this before recently. She jumped to the bottom of the note. It included a formal signature from Kelinda White. Yes, she knew where she'd seen this printing before.

50

With Kelly's note in hand, Cynthia made her way downstairs to the evidence room. Of course, it was locked. She'd hoped to take a look at the mysterious note she'd received the night Linda was attacked. Maybe it was still on Randy's desk? She went back to the main floor just as Hack was coming down the hall from her office.

"Doll, I'm so glad I caught you."

"Sorry, Wanda told me you were looking for me. What's up?" Cynthia kept marching straight for her office, and Hack spun on his heels to keep pace with her.

"We got Paul's phone. That guy was a moron."

Cynthia gave Hack a look that said, "Tell me something I don't know."

"All his raw footage is still on it." Hack pushed his yellow glasses out of his eyes and up on his forehead. The skin around his eyes seemed lighter than everywhere else on his face, giving his face a sort of reverse raccoon appearance. Wow, could computer screens do that?

Cynthia raised her eyebrows. "Well, he as much as admitted to killing Maris last night."

"Yes, but now we have actual footage. The guy was sick."

"Not going to argue with you on that."

"There was another woman there that night. An older woman. A stellar dresser with long hair. She witnessed the whole thing." Vivian, no doubt. "I sent you anything I thought might be relevant. I'll be logging the phone into evidence as soon as I can find a gatekeeper."

"Thanks, Hack."

"You got it, doll." He tapped her desk. "Hang in there," he said, then pulled his yellow shades back down over his eyes and glided out of her office and down the hall.

Cynthia was still holding Kelly's letter. She'd have to check Randy's office for the note she'd given him the morning after Linda had ended up in the hospital, so she strode down the hall. Nothing had changed. Papers were strewn all over the surface of Randy's desk as usual. The collection of coffee cups seemed to have grown. She lifted a couple of them and carefully peeked under some of the papers. The note was under the third stack of papers she moved. She didn't have to be a handwriting expert to see Kelly had written it. No wonder she kept asking about Linda.

She took the note and Kelly's letter back to her office, pausing at the spot in the hall where she'd crouched next to Ben last night. Nobody would be the wiser that anything had happened there.

Back in her office, she was distracted by thoughts of going home and crawling into bed, but managed to continue working on her report. She also thought about Kelly and Christian and how hard it must be for Kelly looking after her brother. Cynthia stuck Kelly's warning note in her pocket. Obviously, Randy had never entered it into evidence. There was no reason to cast any suspicion on Kelly. The statement Kelly had written and left for Cynthia was exactly as Cynthia had expected—what they'd discussed that morning. Surely, Kelly wouldn't be able to continue her side programming gigs if word got out about how she'd hacked into the Cooper Downs network. She'd likely be fired. Cynthia put the statement in her pocket too. She could build a strong case with Sherie's statement. Perhaps the evidence from the network could somehow be pinned on Paul.

She finished her report, highlighting Vivian's role in the theft, including statements from Maris's journal. Randy said Vivian had bribed him. There was no way to tell for sure the money she'd used to bribe him was the money she'd stolen. It seemed pretty coincidental, but coincidences weren't evidence. Things were coming together, but the thing that bothered Cynthia the most was who had collected the money from the fake winning tickets?

Randy had never told her the amount of the bribe, but it would have been substantial for Randy to have taken the bait. Enough to make a serious dent in his debt. Vivian, Paul, and Kelly were all employees of Cooper Downs. It would have looked suspicious for one of them to earn that much extra cash. There had to be someone else involved. Someone who didn't work at Cooper Downs.

Cynthia contemplated all of this, then faced the fact she wasn't going to complete her report today as she'd hoped. She needed more information from Randy. Not only could he tell her more about the bribe, but he'd been close enough to Vivian to see who else she might have been involved with. It would all have to wait, though, because Randy was out, likely following Vivian. Right now, she needed sleep, and she needed to see her son.

51

Cynthia barely made it home without falling asleep at the wheel. The adrenaline from the events of the last twenty-four hours was finally wearing off. She'd just made it in the door and dropped her bag on the dining table when Luke came running for a hug.

"Mommy! Are you done working now?"

"Hi, buddy. Yes, I'm staying home this time. Mommy needs a nap though. You want to read a story with me?" He'd given up on napping months ago, but he'd been through a lot too, and the sleep would do him good.

"I'll go pick a book," he said, running off to his bedroom. Mom and Dad were in the living room watching TV, the volume low.

"Thanks for bringing Luke home," Cynthia said.

"You do what you've got to do, dear." Mom said.

"We're not going anywhere," Dad said, finishing Mom's sentence. Gayle and Bob to the rescue as usual.

"We're fine," Cynthia said, starting to cry. She'd forgotten to stop by the hospital and visit Linda. Mom was by her side in a heartbeat with a firm hug. Cynthia cried harder.

"It's okay not to be fine," Mom said.

"I know. I've been through this before, remember."

"Of course, dear. Of course." Although she couldn't see anything through her tears, Cynthia sensed Mom had looked at Dad with concern.

Cynthia jerked her head up. "I need to call Linda." She wiped the tears from her cheeks, walked to the table, and took her phone out of her bag. "She texted me earlier and I said I'd stop by. I didn't clue in that she must have her phone back." She started entering Linda's number, and her phone auto-completed it from her contacts list.

"Cyn? Thank God. I've been so worried about you."

"I'm sorry. I was trying to wrap things up at the station and completely lost track of time. I know I said I'd stop by, but I need some sleep."

"Of course you do. Argh! I can't believe I'm stuck here while you're going through all this. I'm going to find someone to let me out of here."

Cynthia laughed as she imagined how much of a pain Linda was as a patient. "You need to take care of yourself. I'll be fine. Mom and Dad are here."

"Okay. I'm glad. You get some rest and I'll see you soon, okay?"

"Of course."

"Even though I'm stuck here, you know you can call me anytime, right?"

"I do."

"All right. Maybe I'll have a nap too. There's not much else to do around here."

"You should. I'll talk to you soon," Cynthia said.

"Love you."

"Love you too." Cynthia turned off her phone so it wouldn't wake her while she was napping and put it on the table. Luke came out of his room with a Dr. Seuss book. At least Cynthia could be sure she wouldn't fall asleep while concentrating on that tongue twister.

"Ready, Mommy?"

"Yes."

Even though it was only afternoon, Cynthia told Luke to say goodnight to Grandma and Grandpa. Luke did just that, and they headed into Cynthia's room. Cynthia left the door open a crack. She never liked being completely cut off from the rest of the house.

***

Sometime around dinner, there was a faint knock on Cynthia's bedroom door, and she felt Luke get out of bed. She tried to open her eyes, but her body wanted to stay unconscious a little while longer. She rolled over and cracked her eyes open.

"Cynthia?"

"Mom?"

"There's someone here to see you. It's the detective. Should I tell him to come back another time?"

She wanted to say yes, but her curiosity got the better of her.

"No, it's okay. I'll be right out."

When Cynthia saw Randy, he was standing by her back door. "I told him to sit," Mom said. "But he insisted on waiting for you." Cynthia pursed her lips but managed a half-assed smile and shook her head. Randy had his arms full. A giant bouquet of flowers in one hand and a bag of takeout in the other. "Your father and I will take Luke to get a bite to eat so you two can talk."

"Thanks, Mom." She was sure Randy was there to apologize some more, and she would rather have that conversation in private.

"These are for you," Randy said, and handed Cynthia the flowers after her family had left. She had to admit they were gorgeous. "With my condolences." Randy avoided eye contact as Cynthia took the flowers and searched her cupboards for a vase large enough to hold them.

Randy held up the takeout bag. "I hope you like Chinese," he said as he placed the bag on the table.

Chinese. The last meal she'd shared with Ben. Her stomach turned a little. She took a seat at the table and gestured for Randy to do the same. He shook his head.

"I don't want to keep you. I just wanted you to know I'm resigning as soon as we arrest Vivian."

"Something about this whole thing doesn't make sense to me," Cynthia said, still a little groggy from her nap.

"I already told you why I took the bribe," said Randy.

"Not that." Cynthia's tone was dry. "How did Vivian and Paul cash those tickets without drawing any attention to themselves?"

She purposely left Kelly's name out. "They had to have had someone else working with them. Someone who didn't work at Cooper Downs. As employees, they certainly wouldn't be allowed to gamble there."

"Vivian is an expert in reading people. She'd seen me at the casino many times before approaching me to make a deal. She'd known when I was at my weakest. She likely did the same with whoever was helping them. It probably wasn't just one person, and I can guarantee she wasn't the one who approached them. Probably got Paul to do it. She's too smooth to risk exposing herself."

Cynthia suddenly had a moment of clarity. "What if the only reason Paul went to work at Cooper Downs was to carry out Vivian's plan? If that's true, then they've been stealing from Cooper Downs for years." So much for nailing Cooper Downs to the wall as Linda had wanted. They were a victim too. As much as Cynthia wanted to wrap up this case and move on, she knew she needed to conduct a complete audit on the racetrack winnings from the time Paul started working there. She was sure she'd find more duplicate ticket numbers.

"What did Vivian bribe you with?" Cynthia didn't care she was getting personal. "How much did she offer you?" Randy had become personally involved in this case the minute he agreed to Vivian's proposal.

"One-hundred thousand." Randy looked as if he wanted to say more, to try and explain his behaviour again. Instead, he looked away.

"The three tickets Maris found only totalled thirty-two thousand. Do you think the bribe money was money they'd stolen?"

"I'm not sure how else she would have gotten that kind of money. But I suppose it's possible she used her life savings to protect her son."

"Based on what Maris wrote in her journal, Vivian was making money under the table. She hosted elaborate parties for the horse owners. Maris didn't write any specific details, but from what she did write, it seemed like she was expected to do whatever the horse owners paid her to do. Maybe Vivian did the same?"

"It wouldn't surprise me," Randy said, still standing.

"I'll head back to Cooper Downs in the morning. Check the sales journals from the time Paul started."

"Why don't you make it Monday? It's not like anyone's going to destroy the evidence tomorrow. If that was part of the plan, they would have covered their tracks the minute you started investigating. You know we've got a tracker on Vivian, right? I planted it in her cellphone case. She's going to screw up sooner or later, especially since she just lost her son. She can't be thinking clearly." Randy stepped in the direction of the door. Relief flooded Cynthia's body.

"No, but Warren mentioned the tracker. I'll let you know what I find out." Cynthia thought about standing to see Randy out, but she didn't.

"Cynthia, I'm so—"

"I know." She cut him off. She'd already been reminded of Ben more in the last thirty minutes than she'd have liked.

After Randy left, she dialed her voicemail and listened to the last message Ben had left for her. She always deleted her messages after she listened to them, but this one somehow remained. She listened to it a few more times, then saved it again.

52

Cynthia called Sherie first thing the next morning.

"Good morning, Cynthia. Are you feeling better today?" Sherie sounded quite chipper considering she was running the Cooper Downs accounting department on her own right now.

"I'm doing all right," she said, but Cynthia hadn't taken the time to think about how she actually felt. She'd woken up with a plan—find out who'd cashed the fraudulent tickets then check in with Ben's family and see how they were doing. "Could you do me a favour, Sherie?"

"Of course. Whatever you need."

"Can you meet me at Cooper Downs today? I need to check a few more things."

"Sure. I'm going in later to finish the payroll since no one has heard hide nor hair from Vivian. Employees don't take kindly to being paid late. I'll be there at 1:00 p.m. for a couple hours."

"Thanks, Sherie. I'll see you then."

Cynthia ended the call and put her phone on the kitchen table. Luke was playing with his cars in the living room. She'd finally convinced Mom and Dad that she and Luke would be fine on their own for the night, but she expected Mom to call any minute. She strolled over to Luke and crouched down.

"Why don't you put your cars away, and we'll go see Auntie Linda?"

"Okay." Luke started cleaning up. Cynthia was thankful he was always so agreeable. It probably wouldn't last, but she was going to enjoy it while she could. She thought about Ben's friend, Ryan. She was glad he had waited at the hospital for her the night Ben had died. Ben hadn't been close with his family, and she hadn't met them until Ryan had introduced them at the hospital that night.

Now was as good a time as any to check in on him. She dialed his number and waited for him to answer, not sure what she was going to say.

"Hello?"

"Hi, Ryan. It's Cynthia."

"Oh . . . Cynthia." Something sounded off in his voice.

"I wanted to thank you again for waiting at the hospital for me. How are you hanging in there?"

"As good as can be expected, I guess. Look . . . I don't know how to tell you this."

Cynthia's mind immediately went to Ben's family.

"It's about Ben's service," Ryan said.

"They don't want me there, do they?"

"I'm sorry, Cynthia. Logically, they know it wasn't your fault, but—"

"It's okay. You don't have to explain. I'd probably feel the same if I was in their position."

"Why don't we grab a drink sometime? Have our own tribute?"

"That sounds nice. When's the service?" she asked.

"Tuesday."

"Thanks, Ryan. I'm here if you need me."

"Likewise, Cynthia. Thanks for the call."

Cynthia tucked her phone in her purse and dabbed the tears from the corners of her eyes before turning to Luke.

"Ready to go?"

***

After they had visited Linda at the hospital, Cynthia and Luke stopped for lunch with Mom and Dad. Cynthia left Luke with them while she went to meet Sherie at Cooper Downs. She poured over the ticket records and found another half-dozen duplicate ticket numbers going back two years, about the time when Paul had started working there. She debated asking Hack to check back that far for network breaches and ticket tampering, but hesitated, knowing it would lead to Kelly.

Every single ticket had been cashed by a different person. Most of the amounts were under five-thousand dollars. It wasn't until the three tickets Maris discovered that the amounts jumped to ten-thousand or more. Someone must have gotten greedy. Cynthia made a note of the prize winners. She'd have Hack check their backgrounds.

***

Back at the office, Cynthia still contemplated asking Hack to go back a couple years and check for network breaches in the Cooper Downs system. She decided to wait and see if Randy's plan for Vivian worked out. Instead, she composed an email to Warren letting him know she'd be taking some time off. She finally felt she'd done all she could for now.

53

It was a grey day. The cemetery was quiet except for the family and friends attending Ben's service. Beautiful, neatly trimmed grass carpeted the ground, and moss grew on some of the headstones. The rain had lasted all night, making the grass appear greener than it had in a long time, and there was no chance of it letting up anytime soon.

Cynthia sat on the ground with her legs outstretched in front of her and her back against the grave marker that read, "Jason Travis Webber, June 3, 1983 - February 4, 2016. Dedicated father, loving husband." Cynthia uncrossed her legs, paying no attention to the pool of water forming on the garbage bag she was using as a seat. She hung her head, lost in thought. The rain mixed with the tears flowing down her face. She wasn't sure if it was a raindrop or a tear that dripped off the end of her nose and onto her lap. Her hair hung like a wet mop over her shoulders, and her funeral clothes were so soaked they'd long since given up any hope of warmth. She'd stopped shivering long ago. The numbness protected her from the cold.

"Hey." She heard a familiar voice and looked up just as Linda tapped her knee-high boot with the toe of her own boot. "Thought I might find you here."

Cynthia's eyes smiled but her mouth didn't. "They let you out?" She tried to will her body to stand so she could hug her friend, but it wouldn't. "Are you supposed to be driving?" she asked. Linda was alone and her white Toyota was parked just down the hill.

"Clean bill of health," Linda said, sitting cross-legged next to Cynthia. "You going to join them?" she said, motioning to the congregation of Ben's family and friends.

"I don't think I can," Cynthia replied. She leaned her head against Jason's gravestone.

"It doesn't matter what his family said. If you want to go, then go."

"You know that's not my style," Cynthia said. She pictured Ben's face. "I told him I loved him, but I think he was already dead," Cynthia sobbed as she buried her head in her friend's shoulder. Linda put a hand on Cynthia's drenched head then laid it to rest on Cynthia's arm after giving her a little squeeze.

"Did you?" Linda asked. "Love him, I mean."

"I wanted to, but . . . he wasn't Jason."

"Nobody's ever going to take Jason's place, but you deserve to love again." Linda rested her head on Cynthia's and squeezed her friend again.

"Will I ever get over him?"

"Jason?"

"Yeah."

"Probably not. The older Luke gets, the more he'll remind you of his father, and that's okay."

Cynthia let out another sob, muffled by Linda's shoulder.

"I'm so sorry you had to go through that again. Is there someone you can talk to? A psychologist or something?"

Cynthia looked up at her friend and saw her eyes were also glistening with tears. It would be good to talk to somebody. The department would probably insist on it after all she'd been through.

"I've been waiting for the service to finish so I can say goodbye," she said through chattering teeth.

"You can do that any time. Why don't we get you warmed up?" Linda asked, rising to her feet and extending a hand to Cynthia. She pulled her friend to her feet. "We can get your car later. Let me drive you home."

"Are you sure your doctors said you could drive? I'll be fine, you know."

"I know you'll be fine, but you most certainly aren't fine right now. How long have you been sitting out here anyway?"

Cynthia shook her head and shrugged her shoulders. "I have no idea what time it is." The women headed down the hill arm in arm in the direction of Linda's Tercel. When they got to the car, Linda held the door open for Cynthia. She got in the car and glanced back at the top of the hill, the gathering for Ben barely visible. She watched Ben's family and friends shrink out of view as Linda maneuvered the Tercel out of the cemetery and in the direction of her home. She closed her eyes as tears fell down her cheeks and wished the events of the past week had all been a bad dream.

54

May 5, 2018, Woodbine Racetrack, Ontario

A tall, vivacious woman wearing dark sunglasses weaved her way through the crowd. Her flowing auburn hair fell halfway down her back and sashayed from side to side in sync with her curvy hips as she walked. She wore a large floppy hat with royal purple matching gloves and a lightweight purple raincoat slung over her forearm. Her low-cut black dress speckled with purple flowers ensured she received ample looks from the single men in the crowd. Many married men noticed her too.

She walked up to the betting window. "One-thousand on Justify."

"Excuse me, ma'am?"

"You heard me." She slapped down ten hundred-dollar bills. The teller at the wager window counted the bills by hand then ran them through the bill counter for confirmation. She waved each bill through the counterfeit machine.

"You'll have to step aside please, ma'am, while we check everything over."

"There's nothing wrong with the money," Vivian said.

"It's just protocol." The teller waved her hand at the next person in line. "Next, please."

Vivian huffed and stepped aside, looking anxiously at the other patrons. She watched the teller help several betters, each time expecting to be waved back to the wicket to complete her transaction. A security guard appeared at her side seemingly from out of nowhere.

"Vivian Lennings?"

She hadn't given her name to the teller yet and wondered how the guard knew who she was. She gave him an uneasy yet affirmative nod.

"Come with me, please." The guard lightly placed his hand on her back to guide her out of the lines of people waiting to purchase their tickets.

She glanced around, hoping for a quick exit, but all she saw were more security guards. They were everywhere, their white and black uniforms accentuating every exit like well-placed accessories. Once away from the excitement and noise of the anxious betters, Vivian asked the guard where they were going and what this was about.

"There's a problem with your bet," he said, as he guided her into a meeting room.

"Hello, Vivian," came a familiar voice.

"Randy? I thought you were in jail?" Vivian's face flushed with nerves, and she cursed herself under her breath.

"Have a seat," Randy said, gesturing to the empty chair at the meeting table and ignoring Vivian's question. Randy sat between an official-looking man in a suit and Officer Warren Scott. Vivian took the empty seat while the guard who had escorted her closed the door and remained standing next to it.

"What's this about? I don't want to miss the race." Vivian looked at the man in the suit. "And what's he doing here?" she asked, looking at Randy.

"I'm Detective Hunter with the Toronto Police Service," the suit said. "I've been working with Detective Bain on your case."

Vivian raised her eyebrows. "My case?"

"It appears your money's no good."

"That's ridiculous. There's nothing wrong with my money," she said.

"We ran it through our machine, and it appears it's counterfeit."

Vivian screwed up her face. "That's ridiculous. Do you think I have a printing press in my spare room?" Vivian's tone was condescending.

"We'll need to investigate to find out for ourselves." It was Detective Hunter's turn to raise his eyebrows. "You're welcome to call your lawyer."

Vivian turned to Randy. "You!" She inhaled a sharp breath through pursed lips. "You did this!"

"If you're referring to tracking you down and enlisting the help of Detective Hunter here, then yes, I did this." Randy's mouth formed a sly half smile.

"I thought it was a bit odd your only son died, and you were nowhere to be found. It wasn't difficult to figure out you were up to something."

"My son was an imbecile. I gave up everything for him." Vivian tried to contain her emotions, but they had been bottled up for far too long. "I could have had a career as a jockey before I got pregnant. Do you know how hard that is for a woman? Let alone one of my . . . size?" She hated to imply there was anything wrong with her size, but she was large for a jockey.

The men in the room remained silent, eyes wide, waiting for Vivian to oust herself.

"I was happy to give it all up. Constantly watching what I ate and training. Paul was everything to me. And then he grew up into an ungrateful bastard. I didn't realize how bad he was until I saw what he did to Maris. All I'd wanted to do was ask her to keep quiet about the special parties I hosted. I didn't want her to die."

Vivian held her breath, trying not to cry.

"Why bribe me to protect him then?" asked Randy.

"I wouldn't expect you to understand. A parent does what they have to."

Randy looked like he was about to slam his hand down on the table but caught himself at the last second. "Try me," he said.

"Forget it. I'm not falling for your tricks. I want my lawyer."

"Then answer this," Randy said. He seemed determined to get more out of Vivian even though she'd already asked for a lawyer. "How did you cash all those tickets? We know there was more than what Maris found."

"A single mother comes to rely on the kindness of strangers." Vivian's answer left Randy and Warren looking at each other with furrowed brows.

"You got strangers to cash the tickets?" Randy asked.

"A racetrack is an easy place to find a person down on their luck willing to split the profits of a winning ticket." Vivian glared at Randy, then she raised her chin a little. "The trick is to find some poor sap so desperate he'd do anything for you without telling your secret."

Vivian lowered her head but kept her gaze fixed on Randy, batting her thick fake lashes. "I guess I pegged you wrong, Detective."

55

Cynthia and Linda sat at the dining room table in Cynthia's three-bedroom house, laughing and playing with Luke.

"Do you have any sharks?" Luke asked.

Linda made a funny face and shook her head. "Sorry, my friend. Go fish."

Cynthia saw Warren through the kitchen window. She got up from the table as Warren knocked softly on the door.

"Who is it, Mommy?"

"It's Officer Scott," Cynthia replied as she opened the door for Warren.

"Hi, Cynthia. I'm sorry to bother you at home, but I have some important updates on the Cooper Downs case."

"Come in," she said, eyeing Linda.

"Hey, Luke, why don't we go play with your cars?" Linda knew Luke had an ever-growing collection in his room, and he was always eager to show it off.

"Okay," Luke said, climbing down from the dining chair that was still too big for his four-year old frame.

Linda nodded to Warren as she and Luke left the room. Warren reciprocated with a nod of his own.

"I'm sorry, Cynthia. I know you're still on bereavement leave, but—"

"It's okay. Have a seat." She gestured to the chair closest to the door, and Warren sat.

"I wanted to let you know Vivian Lennings is in custody in Toronto. Randy and I apprehended her at Woodbine Racetrack where she tried to place a bet using counterfeit cash."

"Wow," was all Cynthia could manage.

"There's something else." Warren paused, his eye contact unwavering.

Shit. She thought about Kelly's note and statement she had shredded and how she may have left a few things out of her report. He knows.

"I know you're supposed to come back to work later this week," he continued. "But I think it might be better if you didn't."

"I . . ." Cynthia grasped at the words to explain the indiscretions she'd taken when filing the Cooper Downs report. She sucked in some air, hoping it might cool the burning sensation in her cheeks.

"A member of the Canadian Chartered Professional Accountants' investigative board called me."

Cynthia scrunched up her eyebrows trying to figure out what the CPA organization had to do with the Cooper Downs case.

"They've been continuing their investigation of David Jerew. It appears many of his Calgary clients were involved in criminal activity, and they've asked us to get involved."

"I'm not surprised. That guy turned out to be a real piece of work." Although the thought of David Jerew made Cynthia's stomach turn, she was relieved at the direction the conversation was headed. "Did they need to talk to me again about my involvement with the PPC case?"

"No, actually. I'm not sure how to tell you this . . ."

Just get to the point already, Warren.

". . . it appears your husband, Jason, was working on one of David's files when he died. Do you remember that?"

"No. Unless we were working on the same file, we didn't share many client details."

Warren rested his elbow on the table and hung his head for a second on his hand. When he raised his head, his dark brown eyes met Cynthia's with intensity.

"There's a possibility Jason's death wasn't an accident."

"What? That's ridiculous." This is not how Cynthia had seen this conversation going. "He hit a patch of ice and slid into oncoming traffic."

"I just thought you should know. The federal CPA organization uncovered some suspicious records while looking into your old boss. It looks like the last audit Jason worked on involved some serious organized crime."

Cynthia's mouth gaped, and she continued to look at Warren, but all she saw was a blur. It didn't make any sense.

"We're going to partner with CPA and see what we can find out. But in the meantime, it's best if you and your family lie low for a while. If the mob is watching you, it might not be good for them to see you coming to the station."

"Jesus. The *mob*," was all Cynthia could squeak out.

"Cynthia," Warren said, touching her arm. "Are you all right?"

"She'll be fine."

Warren looked up to see Linda leaning against the wall, her arms crossed over her chest.

"How much of that did you hear?"

"Enough to know Cynthia and Luke might be in danger." She looked at Cynthia, who was questioning Linda with her eyes. "He's in the bathroom," she said. Cynthia closed her eyes, and when she opened them, Linda was sitting beside her at the table.

"It doesn't change anything. Jason's still dead. Ben's dead. Jesus, Warren, you might want to get out of here before something happens to you too," Cynthia said.

"None of that was your fault." Linda was quick to comfort her friend.

Warren stood. "I'll be in touch. We'll get to the bottom of this."

Cynthia stood as well while Warren walked the few feet from her table to the back door. "I'm sorry about the timing of all this," he said.

"It's fine. I know you're just doing your job."

He said his goodbyes to Linda—and Luke, who'd just come out of the bathroom—then stepped outside. Cynthia closed the door as Linda stepped towards her and put her arms around her. She felt comforted knowing Linda had overheard Warren. All that mattered to Cynthia now was that she and Luke were safe, and she intended to keep them that way. She was going to need a gun after all.